LOGAN'S GUN

~~hn Dog Crandal and his gang of
~s ~ttack the ranch belonging to
~~ and his pard, Randy, Logan
~n his Colt Lightning and swears
~ the down-and-out pair reach
~prings they bump into an old pal,
who offers them a lifeline
~ his stagecoach business. Apart from
~ murderous stage robbers, Logan
hands full dealing with Quinn's
~ate, who has the hots for him.
~og Crandal and his thugs
~ Quinns' home. Can Logan meet
in single combat and deal with
~rossing treachery?

LOGAN'S GUN

LOGAN'S GUN

by

John Dyson

Dales Large Print Books
Long Preston, North Yorkshire,
BD23 4ND, England.

British Library Cataloguing in Publication Data.

Dyson, John
   Logan's gun.

   A catalogue record of this book is
   available from the British Library

   ISBN   978-1-84262-678-8 pbk

First published in Great Britain 2008 by Robert Hale Limited

Copyright © John Dyson 2008

Cover illustration © Gordon Crabb by arrangement with
Alison Eldred

The right of John Dyson to be identified as the author of this
work has been asserted by him in accordance with the
Copyright, Designs and Patents Act, 1988

Published in Large Print 2009 by arrangement with
Robert Hale Ltd.

Dales Large Print is an imprint of Library Magna Books Ltd.

Printed and bound in Great Britain by
T.J. (International) Ltd., Cornwall, PL28 8RW

ONE

The air was sucked out of Logan's body as the stallion, Satan, kicked for the sky. One … two … three big bucks as the rancher hung on, one-handed, slapping his hat, whooping with excitement, daring the black beast to do his worst.

An older man by some thirty years, Randy Newbolt, chuckled as he watched, corralside. 'I can still see too much daylight 'tween ya pants an' the saddle.'

Josh Logan gritted his teeth as the powerful brute went into a series of spins, frantic to get this thing off his back. When Satan's hoofs hit the deck it jarred every bone in Logan's body. The horse, however, seemed to sense that this time he wasn't going to win. Suddenly, he came to a halt and stood, eyes rolling, his sweat-flecked body shuddering.

'Steady,' Josh crooned, holding his bridle tight, feeling the power of the stallion between his thighs. 'It ain' no use buckin'. You gotta learn who's boss.'

'Jeez!' Randy gave a whistle of awe. 'I think you finally got him tamed.'

'Yeah,' the rider murmured, easing Satan into a steady trot around the corral. 'He ain't gonna be no trouble no more.'

It was the triumphant conclusion to a long battle. They had trapped the stallion and his harem of wild mares and fillies in a box canyon out on the Staked Plains. A rope around his neck, they had dragged him back a hundred miles, the females following their leader, to this small ranch amid the bleak sage-blue scarpland on the eastern border of New Mexico.

The mares hadn't proved much trouble to tame, but Satan had struggled and kicked in a battle for supremacy that had gone on these past three days.

'I sure am tired of gittin' tossed back an' forth like a rag doll.' The tall, lean Texan eased himself down from the saddle and gentled the stallion's neck, soothing him. He took the harsh spade bit from Satan's mouth and set him free. 'You're gonna be OK now, boy.'

'Ain't he a proud beauty?' Randy opined, as the stallion skittered away. 'We'll git a hundred dollars fer him at Fort Stanton.'

Randy Newbolt had a face like hewn mahogany beneath the wind-bent brim of his hat, which he rarely removed. When he did his bald cranium was as white as a hard-boiled egg. He appeared the archetypal frontiersman, with his walrus moustache, red bandanna, cross-over canvas shirt, and flapping batwing chaps. 'I was born in the saddle,' he would say to explain his bowed legs. 'That's where I like to be.'

He had teamed up with the young Texan on a cattle drive across parched lands and on up the Pecos. They had fought off Comanches, sided each other in troubles, and stuck together a long while. Tired of working for others, six months previously they had homesteaded this land along the rugged Alamosa Creek.

'I dunno about selling him,' Logan mused. 'He'd make me a fine saddle horse.'

Randy scratched at what hair he had straggling down from the back of his head and slapped his hat back on. 'That weren't the idee.'

'You ain't had to friggin' ride him. Three days battling has given me a bond with that critter. Don't gimme that look. All them mares and fillies'll be sure'n fetch twenty dollars each.'

Theirs was an easygoing partnership, but Newbolt generally deferred to the younger man. He was in awe of the fact that the young Texan could actually read and write and had a certain civilized charm. Whereas *his* only skills were of survival on the frontier.

'Suit yaself,' he said. 'You're the boss.'

'We're partners.' Logan grinned as he dusted down his faded denim shirt and jeans and ran fingers through his thick flaxen hair.

'But as I'm the one who does most of the work round here I get the bigger share of the vote.'

He ambled towards the ramshackle cabin they called home, jumped up on to the veranda, his boot spurs jingling, and waved towards a larger corral where they had 300 steers and calves rounded up and branded, all ready to move out. 'We'll get at least twelve dollars a head for them at the fort. Don't worry, pal, we ain't gonna starve.'

Randy took a notebook from his shirt pocket, licked a pencil stub and did some figuring. 'Hey, man,' he hooted. 'We could raise four thousand bucks. Can that be right?'

'I told ya there was money in ranching.' Josh eased himself down into an old cane chair and sought his cigarette makings. 'Maybe this time we'll recoup our losses.'

Since being paid off at the end of the cattle drive things hadn't gone too well. They had slogged at gold-mining up at White Oaks but were too late in the stampede to make much profit. They had tried driving stage for Quinn's new company. But a troublesome woman had put paid to that. Logan wanted to get right away, make a success on his own, so he had suggested they try their own ranch. So, here they were, in the back of beyond.

'What wouldn't I give for a glass of cold beer,' he drawled. 'My throat's as dry as dust.'

'Ye'll have to wait 'til we git to Stinkin' Springs for that.' Randy had gone inside and poured them two tin mugs of hot coffee from the pot on the stove. 'This is all we gonna git 'til then.'

'Thanks.' Logan took the scalding mug of black brew. 'Ya know, pard, I got a feelin' this may be the start of something big. One of these days we're gonna be rich as Chisum. First light we'll get these longhorns moving. We'll get a good price from the colonel at the fort. Or at the Mescalero agency. In a week's time we'll be celebrating in Rosie's saloon at Lincoln with money to burn.'

How wrong, he thought afterwards, could a man be? For, as he put the coffee to his lips and squinted out into the flickering sunset, suddenly, about a mile away, on a ridge of sagebrush, a line of darkly silhouetted riders had appeared and were heading towards them, fast.

'What the hell does this bunch want?' he muttered, reaching to loosen the stud of his holster. He gripped the rosewood stock of his .38 calibre Colt Lightning. It was as if a black cloud had appeared to block his ambitions, for each of the riders had a rifle or carbine held in a threatening manner. A shiver of fear ran through him. 'I don't like the look of 'em.'

'Who *are* these dingbats?' Randy began to back into the cabin to grab his own long-barrelled Greener rifle.

'Who knows?' Logan said, as he got to his feet. 'They got the drop on us, that's fer sure.'

Their homestead, adjacent to the edge of the Staked Plains, gave them access to this vast table of grass that stretched for 300 miles down towards Mexico. On the north Texan side of the border lay some big ranches, the LX, the LIT, and others. Winter 'northers', checked by barely a single tree, drove remnants of their herds south-west across the plateau. At first Logan thought the men might be from one of these spreads. But his conscience was clear. The escaped longhorns bred and proliferated, and his stock consisted of previously unbranded young ones. Surely, such fellow-ranchers would have no grudge?

'These scum are bandits,' Randy gritted out, raising his rifle. 'Shall we let 'em have it?'

'Hold your fire.'

Closer and closer the dark horsemen came, charging towards them across the rocky terrain, until they swirled to a halt in a cloud of dust. There were about two dozen of them, hauled in about thirty paces from the cabin in a threatening line.

'OK, boys.' Logan tried to stay calm, for they looked the kind who needed little excuse to shoot them down. 'What do you want?'

14

An evil-looking bunch, they were a mix of Mexicans in huge sombreros and range leathers, strung with *banderillos* of bullets, and shabby, hard-faced Americans, riff-raff of the frontier. They sat in grim silence.

'What do we want?' A muscularly built man, obviously their leader, nudged his mustang forward a few paces. A worn buckskin jacket hung from his big shoulders, open to reveal a once red, now faded woollen vest. A thick gold necklace hung around his neck. A battered hat was slung over his back, and black hair flowed to his shoulders around the coppery planes of a harsh face. This split into a sneering grin. 'What the hell you think we want?' He rubbed thumb and finger together. 'Dollars. Pesos. Cash.'

'You're outa luck, pal,' Randy hooted, aiming the Greener at him. 'Ye've picked the wrong chickens to pluck. We're broke. On our uppers. Penniless. You savvy? So you better git outa here fast.'

The stranger waved his carbine at the nearby corrals of horses and cows. 'You got stock. So you musta got cash.'

'Nope.' The tall Texan's pale-blue eyes glimmered beneath the shadow of his hat brim. 'We sunk all we had into buying this homestead. Those cattle and horses we've brought in outa the wild. This is the Leanin' Ladder ranch. They got our brand. So touch them at your peril, mister.'

'Touch them at our *peril?*' The big man gave a hoot of laughter. 'You don't seem to understand, my friend. I am here to offer you protection from the *bandidos* who roam these wilds. You pay us. We protect you. Your first payment will be all this stock. You go back to work and next time we might not be so hard.'

'Ye're joking,' Randy hooted. 'We've worked our butts off to raise this stock. You lazy good-fer-nothings can git lost.'

'So, you don't want to co-operate with my business proposition?' The *jefe* grinned at them. 'You want a fight? An unwise decision, my friends.' He raised an arm, indicating the line of rifles and carbines, their deadly

16

mouths aimed at them, their owners waiting the order to fire. 'What's it to be?'

'You'll go first,' Randy threatened, cocking the Greener's hammer. 'Ye'll be knocking at the gates of hell.'

'Maybe. But I suggest it would be wiser if you just toss your weapons off the porch down into the dust here in front of me. In fact, we'll give ya to the count of ten.'

'It ain' no use,' Logan whispered. He carefully removed his Lightning from the holster and threw it forward. 'They got us hogtied, Randy.'

He tried to memorize the line of faces for future reference. That's if he was to have any future, which at that moment seemed highly unlikely. Then the leader's dark features struck a chord with him.

'Crandal,' he said. 'I remember you. John Dog Crandal. The murdering spawn of a Fort Worth whore. Raised in her own thievin' ways. The Rangers ran you outa Texas. So this is where you got to?'

'You shut your mouth,' one of the men

growled. 'Shall I kill him, John Dog?'

'No, he's right.' Crandal's gold teeth flashed. 'I sure am one hundred per cent sonuvabitch. My mama was a pig. But, believe me mister; I'm a real swine.'

Suddenly a noose came spinning from one of his sidekicks dropping neatly over Logan's shoulders, whipcord tight, and he was hoisted from his porch to sprawl in the dust. 'Shall we hang him, John Dog?'

'No,' Crandal shouted. 'Give him the chicken run.'

Before Randy could fire in protest Crandal's carbine barked out and Newbolt recoiled, dropping his Greener, clutching his bleeding right arm.

'Aw, hail,' the older man groaned. 'You lousy snakes.'

He watched as his friend was dragged away through the dust, rocks and scrub at a gallop on a tour at ground level of his homestead. When the rider came charging back he saw the strained look on the bloody face of Logan as he gripped the rawhide rope trying to ride the bumps and bounces.

'OK, that's enough,' John Dog shouted. 'We don't want to kill him, do we? Maybe these two fools have learned their lesson. Next time we call they should be more co-operative. Maybe then we will let them keep half of their stock. But this time we take it all.'

'Yee-hagh!' A boot thudded into Logan's ribs and a voice drawled, as his wallet was ripped from his back pocket. 'You hear that, pal?'

'Hey, thassall I got,' Randy protested, as he too was pummelled by two Mexicans, who leapt on to the porch and snatched his billfold from his shirt. He tried to swing a haymaker with his good arm, but a carbine smashed into his jaw and he fell to his knees. 'Now look what you done,' he wailed, as he spat out blood and a tooth.

'A few lousy dollars,' John Dog said, counting the proceeds. 'Fourteen sixty, in fact. We're wasting our time with these losers. What's in the cabin?'

'Nuthin' worth havin', another Mexican grinned. 'A nice big can of kerosene, John Dog. Should make a tidy blaze.'

'Aw, come on, boys, be sports,' Randy groaned. 'Leave us the cabin. We ain't done nuthin' to you.'

'This'll be a lesson for you,' Crandal said. 'Next time you pay cash.'

'Are you joking?' Bloody and bruised, Logan staggered to his feet to face him. 'You scum of the earth won't get another nickel from me, so I wouldn't count on it. You leave them hosses and cattle where they are or it's you who'll pay. I'm warning *you*, Crandal.'

'He sure is lippy, John Dog,' one of his gang yelled, kicking Logan again. 'Shall we break his arms for him, make him see sense?'

'No, not yet. He jest don't understand.' John Dog smiled, magnanimously. 'Listen hard, you two no-accounts. We are offering all the ranchers around here protection. The smaller ones, that is. You pay up and we let you operate in peace. You don't.' He snapped his fingers 'Pouf!'

'Yeah, pouf to you, too, pal,' Randy jeered.

'You listen to me,' Josh Logan gritted out. 'I've told you once. I'll tell you twice. You won't get a cent more outa me. I'm not a man who changes his mind.'

'All right, boys,' Crandal shouted, 'get them longhorns and hosses outa the corrals. There'll be a full moon tonight. It'll be as easy as taking candy from a baby to drive 'em down the crik. Should make a tidy price.'

Yipping and hallooing the gang rode away, kicking down the makeshift corral, herding the cattle out in a bellowing billow of dust, and heading away through Alamosa Creek.

Logan watched them go, watched bitterly as a lariat went spinning over Satan's head, and, biting, kicking, and whinnying he was dragged away after the gang followed by the mares and foals.

John Dog had remained with half a dozen of his swarthy Mexican *compadres* to keep them covered. *'Muchas gracias* for your co-operation, *señors,'* he mockingly called, producing a stick of dynamite from his

21

saddle-bag. He struck a match on his nail and lit the fuse, brandishing it to set it sparking and hissing. 'Let's git outa here, boys.'

His men jeered and hooted, but quickly hauled on their reins, whipping their mounts away. They knew how crazy John Dog Crandal was. The gunman grinned and hurled the dynamite at the cabin.

Josh grabbed hold of Randy by his shirt, pulled him from the veranda and went with him, rolling across the dirt. Then he got to his feet and dragged his partner on with him, to dive for the cover of a horse trough.

Whoompf! The kerosene fed the almighty blast, flames shooting into the air. The heat and power hit them as they ducked down, shielding their faces. Parts of cabin planks which they had laboriously hauled from the sawmill to their chosen site showered down about them. The roaring flames died down a bit, but when the two men took a peek there was little to be seen of their cabin or camp except smouldering remains.

'Just look at that burn,' Randy mumbled.

'All that hard work gone to waste.'

'Yeah.' Logan got to his feet. 'That's another get-rich-quick scheme come to an end. You OK?'

'Yeah.' Randy examined his arm wound. 'Ain't nuthin' to worry about.'

'Yep. At least they didn't kill us. We gotta count small mercies.' Josh picked up his Stetson, dusted himself down. 'Just as well we hitched the saddle hosses up along the valley to graze. We won't have to walk back to town.'

'True. But I'm beginning to wonder if I did right ridin' along of you. It's started to strike me you're jinxed, Logan.'

'It's this territory that's jinxed. It's time honest folk started to fight back.'

TWO

The notorious outlaw, Billy Bonney, might have been gunned down there the previous summer, but Fort Sumner was still the haunt of criminals in 1882. Abandoned by the military in '68 it had been bought by the Maxwell family. They had been joined there not only by law-abiding Mexican sheep-herders, but a ripe selection of bandits, traders, whoremongers, gamblers, whiskey-peddlers, and hardcore fugitives.

John Chisum still ruled his cattle empire, the biggest on the Pecos. Settlers were re-covering from the internecine feuding of the Lincoln County War. But it had not brought an end to the shootings. Rustlers found a ready market for their stolen beeves.

The nationwide publicity given to the Kid had stirred many a young rowdy to emulate his pistol-spinning deeds. The proliferation of weapons, the thirst for whiskey, the arrival on the new railroad to Las Vegas of criminals on the lam from Eastern law-enforcement agencies, made New Mexico a hotbed of crime. Many drifted a hundred miles down the Pecos to the rumbustious fort. Lawmen were reluctant to visit or interfere, for the violence of the gun still ruled this wild land.

'How's y'arm?' Josh Logan enquired of Randy Newbolt as they saddled their broncs in the early dawn beside the still smoulder-ing ashes of their cabin.

'Buzzin'. But it ain' no worse than I've had afore.' Randy had washed the flesh wound in a horse trough and bound it tight with his sweaty bandanna. 'If there'd been half a dozen, you an' me could've taken 'em, but a score is too many for two men.'

'Yep.' Josh had found his Colt Lightning amid the rubble and stuck it back in his holster. 'Maybe there'll be a reckoning one day. What riles me is the thought of Satan. He'll suffer under whip and spur and other tortures men call breaking a critter. He'll turn bad, that's fer sure. I'd jest reached some kinda bond with that horse.'

'You know, I think you're right. All those bastards will do is turn him outlaw. Let's hope he kicks the daylights outa one or two.'

It was a fifteen-mile ride down Alamosa Creek to the nearest outpost of so-called civilization, Stinking Springs, a smattering of ruddy adobes and narrow lanes at the apex of three streams. Originally a Mexican outpost, it had been invaded by a few wandering Americans hoping to make money selling goods, women and whiskey to the cowboys of the Wilcox-Brazil and Yerby ranches.

But it looked much as it was described by one Eastern traveller: 'the dirtiest and filthiest place I have yet visited. The people lack life and energy. The most industrious creatures are the hogs rooting day and night around the houses, creating an intolerable noise and stench.'

'Gawd!' Randy moaned, as they loped in. 'It sure is aptly named! Stinkin' Springs. You can say that agin.'

They let their broncs sup at a filthy waterhole and wandered over to the general store. Amos Adams was leaning on his counter staring into space. 'Give you a loan? You must be crazy. Those gunmen descended on me like a cloud of locusts. Cleaned me out. Food, clothing, boots, barleysugars. Just helped 'emselves to anything they fancied and rifled my cash drawer.'

It was the same in the cantina run by Manuel Lopez. The cattle and horses had left their calling-cards in the street and so had their herders in his bar. It was wrecked. Tables, chairs overturned, bottles smashed. '*Sí*', they had high old time. They say unless I pay they be back to do the same again. No, forgive me, *señors*, I cannot give you credit. I have my family to feed.'

One of the Yerby cowboys swaggered into the cantina, unsteady on his legs. 'You'll find the action along in Peg Leg Fanny's place.

They missed her!' he yelled, pointing down a lane. 'Knock three times. But she don't open up to nobody she don't like the look of.'

Randy's nose was twitching as the scent of liquor led them towards the establishment. It was just a plain adobe block, with shuttered windows and a locked iron door facing on to the street. Round the back was another door with a small iron grille. Muffled sounds of voices and music wafted through. Logan hammered three times with the butt of his revolver. No response. He tried again. *Bang, bang, bang!*

Two red-rimmed eyes about a rosily veined nose beneath a tangle of grey hair peered out. 'You with that mob who passed through early on?'

'No.'

'You lawmen?'

'Who us? No way.'

'Come on in.'

The door was unlocked and a scrawny woman puffing on a curved pipe admitted them. They were hit by a blast of noise from a room jampacked with humanity. A black banjoist in a checked suit and bow tie was plucking his strings, two doxies were screaming with excitement, and cowboys were lined up along a makeshift bar, or crowded around a roulette table. Most had tankards of beer or whiskey in their paws and some looked like they might have been there from the night before.

Fanny shoved through them, her peg leg making her hip swivel beneath her long grey dress. She went behind the bar and shouted to them above the din, 'What's it to be, gents?'

Logan disliked asking favours, but needs must. He stroked his unshaven jaw, leaned over the plank counter and beckoned her closer. 'It's like this,' he said. 'We're down on our luck. To tell the truth, we've been robbed. Lost everything.'

'Aw, no,' the lady wailed. 'Not another coupla deadbeats. Mister, I've had enough of panhandlers. Do I look like a soft touch? On your way. Git outa here. Beat it.'

'My pal here's purty handy with a dish-mop. You got an axe I'll split logs. All we want is a pint of whiskey and a plate of supper.'

Peg Leg Fanny assessed him. 'OK, git out in the yard. I'll call you when you've done enough. Here, you.' She tossed an apron at Randy. 'Put that on. Clear the tables. Get them plates washed.'

Two hours passed before she decreed that they had done enough. In her cramped back kitchen she slopped out venison stew and potatoes into wooden bowls. They filled their bellies and returned to the crowded bar. Peg Leg plonked two large clay pots of home-brewed liquor on the counter. 'Don't hang around long,' she ordered. 'You're occupying valuable space.'

'You're an angel, madam,' Randy crooned. 'A drop of the prairie lightning I bin dreamin' of.'

But when he took a glug he shook his bald head like a stunned dog. 'Hay-zoose!' he cried. 'It blows your damn head off.'

Josh treated it more circumspectly. 'Kicks like a mule. But who's complaining?'

Due to the low ceiling he had to stoop his shoulders, but his eyes lingered on a young brunette perched on a stool at the roulette table. She was attired in the modest manner of the times in a long dress of green silk, pinned by a cameo brooch at the throat. Her cheeks had a natural bloom and needed no powder and rouge, but her full lips were painted crimson and from them drooped a cigarette. 'Place your bets, gents,' she called, as she scooped piles of coloured chips towards her and set the wheel spinning again. As the ivory ball scampered around to its final slot she sang out, 'Twenty-six. *Vingt-six.*'

Glancing around she met Logan's pale-blue eyes and for moments her own dark ones sparkled, warmly, in the candlelight glow. But she quickly returned her attention to her customers. 'Here we go, gents. Who's gonna hit lucky tonight?'

Maybe, Logan thought, with his unshaven

jowls, scratches, cuts, dusty and blood-stained garb, his hair badly in need of a cut, he didn't look a very promising proposition. Or maybe she didn't hobnob with the clientele. She had a remarkably innocent, well-scrubbed look for a girl of her profession. But appearances could be deceptive.

'Ain't no point you fallin' for them pair of laughing eyes,' Randy butted in, reading his thoughts. 'We're broke. You need plenty in your poke to afford that hussy.'

There was a clamour and commotion from the far end of the adobe shack. Through the throng, Logan glimpsed a strongly built man, his three-piece suit tucked into tall boots, whirling one of the *nymphes-de-prairie* in an exaggerated waltz. He was bumping drunkenly into other men spilling their drinks, and it looked like a brawl was about to begin.

'Aw, no,' Josh growled. 'Quinn! Why did we have to bump into him?'

'If there's trouble,' Randy grinned, 'Quinn's bound to be there.'

Quinn had handsome, if brutal, Mexican

looks. His black hair flopped over his brow as he pushed men aside like skittles, roaring, 'Git outa my path.' He waltzed with great abandon their way. Suddenly he saw them and abruptly dropped the dance girl. He staggered forward to slap both hands to the Texan's shoulders, hugging him. 'Josh Logan!'

'That's me. See you're still fond of the ladies and the liquor, Quinn.'

'So, you ain't? Come on, have a drink.'

'Nope,' Logan protested. 'We're just leaving.'

'What? Don't talk crazy. You wouldn't refuse a drink with an ol' *compañero*.' He hauled them both to the bar. 'Gimme a bottle, Peg Leg.'

'How about me, sweetie?' The goodtime gal's chubby face was perspiring freely under its coating of paint. 'You owe me.'

'Aw, git lost.' Quinn shoved a hand into her face. 'This is my old pal, Josh. I ain't seen him in six months. Why'd ya walk out like that, Josh, without even a goodbye?'

'Bottoms up.' Randy hastily filled his tumbler from the bottle. 'I gotta tell ya, Quinn, we cain't buy ya one back.'

'I don't expect you to buy me one,' Quinn yelled. He tossed greenbacks at the beseeching girl. 'I'm loaded. See?'

'What he means is we're temporarily outa funds. The fact is we got robbed at our ranch by a miserable gang of toerags led by John Dog Crandal. He took our hosses, our cows, our last few dollars. Cleaned us out.'

'Crandal?' Quinn suddenly seemed to sober up. 'What did he want?'

'Cash for protection,' Josh scowled. 'When I told him I didn't have nuthin', nor would I give it him if I had, he blew us to smithereens.'

'Dynamite? Yeah, that's Crandal. A little trick of his. Well, at least you stood up to him. Good for you, pal.' Quinn slapped his shoulder and mock-punched him. 'That's the way to deal with Crandal. So, you're stonybroke? Well, that's a laugh. You shoulda stayed with me. I've hit it rich.'

'I'm glad to hear it, Quinn. You allus was a lucky sonuvagun.'

'Yeah,' Quinn growled in his racous voice, still hanging on to Josh, waving the bottle of liquor about. 'I'm loaded. That stage agency we started, I've got the gov'ment contract for the mail. Big income, believe me. Me an' the governor, the state governor at Santa Fe, we're like that.' He grinned widely, holding up two intertwined fingers. 'They're all on the take.'

'You don't say?' Logan shrugged off his arm and took a quaff of the whiskey. 'Kate still with you?'

'Of course she's still with me. Why shouldn't she be? I've bought into a gold mine up at White Oaks. A third interest. Boy, I cain't stop making money. Kate's living like a lady. You should see our new spread. You shoulda stayed with us.'

'Yep. Maybe.' The last time Logan had seen Kate she had been naked beneath him in Quinn's marital bed while he was away in Las Vegas. When he told her he'd had enough, he couldn't go on like that, she had started spittin' and snarling threats like a wild cat.

'I prefer to be my own boss. We gotta be gettin' along now, Quinn.'

'Don't be stupid. You ain't goin' nowhere. You're down and out. Where else you gonna go?'

'We'll get by. Somethang'll turn up.'

'You're coming back with me, *amigo*. No argument. Kate will love to see you. I need you, Josh. I need a good right-hand man I can trust. Tell him, Randy. He can't turn down a chance like this.'

Newbolt shrugged uncomfortably. He was more aware than Quinn, it seemed, of Kate's carryings-on. He glanced at Logan. 'He's the boss. But we could sure do with a leg-up.'

'I've told you,' Logan insisted. 'I like to work for myself.'

'I'll make you a partner. Look, pal' – Quinn pulled a fat wallet from his inside pocket, brandished it under Josh's nose, ruffling a thumb across a wad of notes – 'with you alongside us we can't fail. We need a man who knows what he's doing, a good head on his shoulders, who ain't afraid of hard work. You can run the stage line all on your own.'

Logan noticed a couple of rough *hombres* watching them through the fug of tobacco smoke. 'Put that away, Quinn. You shouldn't flash your cash. It ain't wise. Good to see ya. We'll be on our way now.'

'Allus movin' on,' Quinn roared, hanging on to him. 'You know why you never get anywhere? You're a born drifter. You got the wanderlust. You'll never be a winner like me.'

Logan broke his grip, tossing him away. 'Take it easy on the juice, Quinn. You've had too much. So long.'

'Yeah, go and sleep under a damn cactus amid the ants and pariah dogs, you loser,' Quinn slurred. 'Thass where you belong.'

'Come on, Randy,' Logan said. 'Let's git outa here.'

It was already getting dark outside. 'We

musta been in there longer than I thought.'

'Well, where *are* we gonna sleep?' Randy asked. 'He's got a point.'

'We'll mosey on down the Pecos. Chisum's allus lookin' fer hired hands.'

'What, for thirty a month? Put your life on the line?'

Logan stood at the end of the alley, hesitating, deep in thought, stroking his jaw.

'You having second thoughts?'

'Nope,' he smiled. 'I'm thinking of that li'l croupier gal. I didn't say goodbye.'

'So? You didn't say hello, either.'

'There was somethang about that gal...'

'Aw, Logan, don't go gettin' romantic notions. She's just a whore.'

'Yeah, I guess.'

They were about to turn away when they saw Quinn lurch out of Fanny's and stagger away along the alley in the opposite direction, hanging on to the wall to steady himself.

'He's sure had a skinful.'

But then the shadowy shapes of two men

emerged from the booze joint and followed him. One was swinging what looked like a sock full of lead shot....

Sure enough, they set about the stage owner, one buffaloing him across the back of the neck with the butt of a revolver. Quinn roared defiance and swung at them, but the other footpad's weapon caught him across the temple, knocking him to the floor. They hammered blows into him, pinning him down.

'Hey.' Logan set off at a run, followed by Randy. He caught the sock-swinger by the shoulder as he struggled to get Quinn's wallet, and smashed a hard right into his face. His nose split like a ripe tomato. Logan's left hammered into his ribs and he followed up with another straight right to the jaw. Meanwhile Randy was piling into the other thief, twisting his gun from his grasp.

The mughunters stared at them with horror. Then took to their heels. 'Yeah, you better run, pal,' Logan shouted.

Randy kneeled beside Quinn, examining a

bloody gash at the base of his skull. 'He don't look too good,' he said. Quinn groaned, rolling over, looking up at them. 'Josh, where did you come from? Did they get my cash?'

'No, I got it here.'

'Thanks, Josh,' Quinn mumbled. 'I knew you wouldn't run out on me this time.' He tried to get up but collapsed, falling back, seemingly unconscious. A nasty patch of blood was pooling under his head.

'I'll see if Peg Leg Fanny's got a bowl of water and a bandage,' Randy said.

'Yeah?' Logan stared at Quinn. 'I ain't so sure he ain't just dead drunk.'

There was a bit of a commotion as rubbernecking cowboys came from the drinking joint to take a look. 'Damn fool was asking for trouble,' Fanny said, examining the wallet. 'Carrying this wad around. Which reminds me' – her slick fingers deftly extracted several dollar bills – 'he didn't settle up with me.'

The croupier girl was kneeling, washing the blood away. 'He ought to have stitches in this cut,' she said.

'Just bandage him up, Dawn,' Peg Leg curtly replied. 'He's got a two-horse rig down in the square. We'll put him in it.'

'How's he going to get home?' the girl asked.

Logan had an overwhelming desire to stroke her soft, dark waves of hair as she knelt knee-height. What's a gal like you doing in a place like this? he wanted to ask. But knew it would be a foolish, hackneyed question. Instead, he felt an urge to make a crazy, noble gesture to impress her. 'I'll take him back,' he said.

The croupier girl turned her black, soulful eyes up to him. 'Mr Quinn's lucky he's got a good friend like you.'

He put an arm around her waist as she rose to her feet and for moments she faced him, intimately. 'Aw, it's the least we can do. He's an old pal. The handle's Josh Logan,' he drawled, offering his hand. 'Maybe we'll meet again.'

She met his eyes with a quizzical smile, as

41

he gently caressed her palm. 'Dawn Adamson,' she said. 'Who knows? Perhaps we will.'

'Hey,' Peg Leg Fanny snapped. 'Come on, gals. Everybody back inside. I'm losing business. They'll take care of him.'

'Hey, hang on. Where's he live?' called Logan.

'Down at Roswell,' Fanny sang out. 'It's only a forty-mile drive. You should be there by dawn.'

'Shee-it!' Randy gave an exasperated sigh when they were alone. 'What you playing the good Samaritan fer? I thought you didn't want nuthin' to do with him.'

Logan shrugged. 'We cain't just leave him here.' He didn't notice Quinn open one eye, give a smile of catlike satisfaction, and close it again.

'Gimme a hand to hoist him up, Randy. He's a dead weight.'

A full moon had risen high by the time they reached the Pecos and it was plain from the deep rutted prints of cloven hoofs in the river mud that their stolen cattle had been herded north towards old Fort Sumner. There was little point in following. What could two men do against twenty *viciosos* in that outpost of outlaws? In his mind Logan vowed vengeance one day, but he would have to work out just how to wreak it.

Anyways, they needed to turn south, downriver, to deliver their passenger, Quinn. This was true cattle country, carpeted with grama grass as far as the eye could see, the Pecos plains shimmering in the moonlight. This was the domain of John Chisum who had arrived from Texas in '67 trailing a herd of longhorns. Now his stock had multiplied to 80,000 head and ranged for 150 miles down towards the Texas line. Interlopers on to these public lands were not welcome. But they came, anyway, often with violent results.

The little community of Roswell was an oasis in the heart of the plains at the meeting of the Pecos and the Rio Hondo which flowed down from the dark mass of mountains to the west where the Apaches lurked, through the small township of Lincoln to Roswell. There it was joined by two spring streams. The resulting network of life-giving *acequias* nourished cornfields, fruit orchards and shady cottonwoods.

'Quinn's sure found himself a swell place to have a house,' Randy remarked as they surveyed the settlement under the dawn light. 'This guy musta been born under a lucky star.'

'Yeah,' Logan grunted, non-commitally, as they hauled Quinn into his luxurious – for those parts – residence. 'Let's dump him here.'

THREE

'Say, look what the cat's brought in!'

Logan wasn't sure whether she was referring to him or Quinn. 'Hi, Kate. He's got a bit of a bad head.'

'I bet he has.'

'No,' Randy explained. 'He got jumped in an alley. Lost a lot of blood. He's been out cold on the back of the rig all night. Better put a blanket over him.'

'What, mollycuddle the hard head?' She went across, grabbed Quinn by his thick black hair, twisted his head and took a look at the cut. 'Too bad they didn't make a better job of it. What you two looking for – a reward?'

'Nope, we ain't lookin' fer nuthin',' Logan replied, angrily.

She was a woman older than he, but well-preserved, slim, high-browed, with an arrogant sort of beauty. Her auburn hair was coiffed and curled, and she wore a white silk blouse, a split leather riding-skirt, and neat boots on her shapely legs. She tossed Quinn's head away with a fastidious sniff of her neat nostrils. 'Get a whiff of the whiskey.'

Suddenly her husband came back to life with a roar like a mountain lion. He grabbed her backside and pulled her to him. 'Gimme a kiss, darlin'. Ain'tcha missed me?'

'Like a hole in the head.' She fought away from his rough clutches. 'Stay where y'are. I guess I gotta dose you with black coffee.'

'Look who's here. Josh Logan. And ol' Randy. Ain'tcha pleased I brought 'em back? Get some vittles on, woman. These boys are starvin'. Where's your hospitality? They saved my life. Saved my wallet. Saved my bacon.'

'You don't say?' Kate eyed him sardonically. 'What am I s'posed to play? The devoted li'l wife waiting at home while you go out whoring?'

'I mighta downed some whiskey last

night,' Quinn shouted, hoisting himself out of the rocker. 'But I swear to you I never looked at another woman. Never have. Why should I when I got a woman like you?'

He started stumbling about, clattering a frying-pan, knocking over a can of milk. 'Come on, boys, I'm gonna make you coffee and breakfast. Where's the eggs? Where you keep stuff in this house?'

'Oh, get out of the way, I'll do it.' She avoided his embrace, pushing him away. 'You cause more trouble than you're worth.'

'Yeah, she didn't say that when I bought her that magnificent white thoroughbred for her birthday.' Quinn winked at them and sat down at the table. 'Oh, no, she was mighty grateful that night, I can tell you. She ain't allus like this. A very loving lady is my wife, Kate. Sit down, boys, relax.'

Logan sighed but did as he was bid. 'All we did was bring you home, Quinn. I ain't planning on stayin'.'

'Come on, partner. Don't start that again,' the Mexican growled. 'I need you to run the

47

stage line. I'm too busy up at the mine. To tell the truth I've been having trouble from Crandal, too. I need a coupla guys like you who ain't scared of him.'

'Now he tells us,' Randy exclaimed. 'Mighta known there was a catch to it.'

'Come on.' Quinn caught Logan's arm. 'Some of us have gotta stand up to the likes of him. We can't allow 'em to run us out of the territory. Tell Josh, Kate. We need him.'

'Speak for yourself.' She gave a down-turned grimace as she broke eggs into a pan. 'Me, I don't need any man.'

'Come off it,' Quinn shouted. 'You know you were cut up when he walked out on us. You were like a bear with a sore head mop-ing about for days. Tell him all's forgiven, he's welcome back, Kate.'

'Is that what you really want?' She turned to her husband and met his dark, smoul-dering eyes. Then Logan's more pacific-blue ones, and gave a scoffing smile. 'Welcome back, Josh yoo-ah!'

Quinn made a remarkable recovery and,

after breakfast, proudly showed them how the *casa* had been converted from a terrace of three sturdy adobes. There were his work office, his gun racks, his billiards den, the dining-room with polished table and leather upholstered chairs, and he gave a throaty guffaw as he led them into the master bed-room. 'This is where the action happens!'

'Yeah,' Logan drawled, swallowing bile as he glanced at the satin-covered bed. He was already wishing he hadn't agreed to stay.

He turned to meet Kate's twinkling eyes as she leaned against the doorway. 'What's the big lunk bragging about now?' she asked.

'Guess,' he growled, as the heavy odour of the French perfume she favoured reminded him of times past. He squeezed past her and was shown the stables, outhouses and fields where Quinn's Mexicans laboured. Quinn kicked open the door of a dark, musty shack and said, 'Here's where you two can bunk.'

'Well, thanks,' Randy replied, not without sarcasm, 'but afore we settle in hadn't you better tell us just what you're expecting and how much we git paid?'

'Plenty of time for that. All I want is for you two to run the stage service from the White Oaks mines down through Lincoln to here, then north to Las Vegas. Then back again. The stage and hosses are at White Oaks. We'll ride up and you can get started.'

'What about your regular driver?' Logan asked.

'He walked out on me,' Quinn muttered. 'Just like you. You can't trust nobody these days.'

'*Why* did he walk out?' Josh asked. 'That's what I'd like to know.'

'Aw, he had a bit of trouble from stage robbers. Nuthin' you two cain't handle?'

'You think?' Logan grunted. 'What makes you so sure of that?'

'Because you're good guys,' Quinn roared, swinging his arms around their shoulders and hugging them. 'Here, you need some spending money?' He dug out his wallet, stuffed twenty dollars each into their hands. 'We'll work out the details later.'

'What about the so-called partnership you were tellin' me about?' Logan pressed.

'Doncha worry, Josh. I'll discuss that with Kate. Then we'll go see a lawyer, have it drawn up nice and legal.'

Suddenly Kate burst out of the stable aboard a fine spirited grey mare. 'Ain't you boys ready to head for Lincoln yet? I'm gonna give Blanche a gallop. You can catch up with me.'

She went careering away, heading out of the homestead and up along the bank of the Hondo, kicking up dust.

Quinn watched her go. 'That woman of mine's crazy,' he laughed. 'Come on, boys, we'd better git after her.'

'Aw, no, we been driving your rig all night,' Randy groaned. 'When we gonna have us some shut-eye?'

'There ain't much time for sleep when Kate an' Quinn are around,' Logan said, as they ambled away to unhitch their saddle broncs. 'Now maybe you see why I wasn't so eager to return to these fireworks.'

51

'Cheer up, pardner.' Randy gave a whoop of glee as he swung into his saddle. 'Jest think what we can do with twenty dollars each in Lincoln.'

'You can fergit the wine an' women,' Josh hollered as he rode after him. 'Quinn's expectin' us to drive his damn stage two hundred and fifty miles to Las Vegas. What fer? Peanuts? I don't trust him. Nor that two-timin' wife of his.'

When they reached Lincoln after a fifty-mile ride Quinn booked himself and Kate into the best front room at the Wortley Hotel. Randy and Logan shared a smaller room at the back. They dined together, but in a subdued way, Quinn still suffering either from the crack to his head or a heavy hangover. Logan stayed cool and non-commital to them both. About ten o'clock, Quinn said he was turning in and lurched off upstairs. Kate decided she wanted to take a look at the stars, get a breath of fresh air out on the veranda. There was no mistaking that come-hither look as she stepped out into the night.

'I ain't dancing to her tune no more,' Logan muttered. 'Come on, pal, let's git some sleep. I wanna find the sheriff in the morning 'fore we head out.'

FOUR

'So you lost some cattle and hosses?' Pat Garrett looked a bit of a dude in his four-button brown tweed suit, celluloid collar and tie, as he lounged in his swivel-chair, long legs up on his desk. 'What you expect me to do about it?'

'You're sheriff of Lincoln County, ain'tcha?' Logan said. 'I'm registering a formal complaint. Or do you only look after them who pay you well, like John Chisum?'

Garrett gave a scoffing laugh, his green eyes twinkling, but there was a vicious twist to his thin lips beneath his moustache. 'You got any proof the stock was yourn? Or did you come by it in the usual manner?'

'Our proof was the brands on those critters,' Randy howled at him. 'Our brand, the Leaning Ladder outfit. John Dog

54

Crandal and that scum he rides with stole 'em from under our noses.'

'Anybody killed?'

'Nope,' Josh drawled. 'They got the drop on us.'

'In that case there ain't much I can do. For a start, I never heard of the Leaning Ladder. And for second, I'm too damn busy. I got more important things to do.' The former buffalo hunter stood and stretched, at six feet four towering over Randy, and four inches taller than Logan, too. 'Time for my morning tipple.'

Garrett had been living on his laurels as the killer of Billy the Kid the previous summer, albeit he had ambushed him in a darkened room at Fort Sumner.

'I got news for you, Garrett,' Josh drawled. 'You got an even worse band than the Kid's on your hands now. Crandal and his thugs.'

'The name does ring a bell,' Garrett said with a grin. 'But we've no reports of killings by him in this territory. Killings are what I'm interested in.'

'And reward money?'

Garrett reached for his hat. 'I got an election coming up. I ain't got time for your worries. Crandal's just small fry to me.'

'Mighta known that'd be all the help we would get,' Logan muttered, unhitching his pinto. 'We better git movin', Randy. They're waiting.'

The Quinns were coming from the Wortley Hotel, looking across the road at them as they mounted their own horses.

'You boys working for Quinn?' Garrett asked.

'Nope, we're partners,' Randy put in. 'We're reorganizing the stage line.'

'Best of luck to you,' Garrett smiled. 'Tell you what, boys, I could swear you in as deputies, then you could legally gun down this Crandal if you cross paths again. That's iffen he don't kill you first.'

'No thanks,' Logan gritted out. 'We've got enough on our hands driving the damn stage.'

Garret gave a hoarse laugh. 'Well, don't

expect me to do your killing for you.'

'I won't,' Logan replied.

They had to ride another forty-five miles by wagon road, which wound up into the mountains beneath the flat hump of the 3,000-feet El Capitan peak, before they reached the bustling mining camp.

White Oaks had boomed after gold was discovered there in 1869. Pitch-roofed cabins climbed up the mountainsides and the town's ten saloons and gambling houses vibrated with life day and night.

As soon as they arrived in the late afternoon Quinn strode off to attend to his mining interests, while Josh and Randy took a look at the sturdy Concord coach and horses in the corral at Quinn's livery stables.

'Everything seems OK this end,' Logan said. 'I wonder what the catch is?'

All four met up for a dinner of Porterhouse steaks and pumpkin pie, washed down with California wine, in the back room of the town's top hotel, the Golden Garter.

'Before you get pie-eyed,' Logan said, 'I'm gonna need some ready cash to cover expenses on this trip. We may well need to buy extra horses for the way stations.'

'Sure, you get everything organized, Josh,' Quinn replied. 'How much you want?'

'Two hundred should do. I'll get receipts for any purchases.'

Quinn dug out his wallet and slapped the cash on the table for him. 'Drink up, pardner,' he shouted, splashing the wine about. 'Say, while you're gone I'll get the sign repainted. Quinn and Logan Express Stage Lines. How's that sound? *Salud!* to us, *amigo.*'

Through narrowed eyes Kate watched her husband getting more and more inebriated, her gaze switching from him to Logan and back again. Sometimes she reminded Josh of a wildcat up a tree waiting to pounce.

Quinn beckoned him closer, speaking in a husky whisper. 'You got a ver' important strongbox to carry in the morning. Bars of gold bullion. Five thousand dollars' worth for delivery to the railroad at Las Vegas. I'm putting my trust in you to get it there, Josh.'

'Oh, yeah? I mighta known. That's a helluva responsibility, Quinn.'

'Wassa matter? Can't you handle it?'

'We can only try. Anybody else got wind of this?'

''Course not. Top secret. Look, do you wanna be my partner or not?'

'I said we'll give it a try.' Logan got to his feet looking slightly disgruntled. 'I'm gonna stretch my legs, see the town, maybe sit in a game of monte.'

'Sure, we'll come, too.'

'No thanks, I prefer my own company tonight. See y'all in the morning.'

'What's the matter with him?' Quinn growled. 'I've rescued him from the gutter, given him my cash, set him up in business, bought him dinner. What's the chip on his shoulder? Does he think he's too good for us?'

'Oh, you,' Kate scolded. 'You and your bluster. You'd scare anybody off.'

Randy made a downturned grimace. 'You don't wanna worry about Josh. He's jest a bit of a lone wolf at times.'

When Logan got back to the livery where he and Randy were bedding down above the horses it must have been about two in the morning. 'Hi, Josh,' a voice purred, as he stepped through the door.

'Kate!' She took him by surprise as she caught hold of him, pulled him into her perfumed embrace. 'What you doing here?'

'What you think I'm doing here?'

'Where's Quinn?'

'That lunkhead. Forget about him.' Kate held on to him, peering expectantly up into his face, her lips half-open, waiting to be kissed. 'It's you I want, darling. I knew you'd come back.'

Logan tried to restrain her, but she hung on tight, her eyes glinting feverishly in the moonlight.

'It's over, Kate. I'm just here to do a job.'

'Over? It's never over.' Her nails clawed

into his arms through his shirt. 'I'm the one who says it's over. You still love me, Josh. You know you do.'

'You're married, Kate. Don't that mean anything to you?'

'No, it don't. I don't care. He doesn't know anything. There's no need to be worried about him, darling. He was drunk again, snoring like a pig in bed when I left him. Kiss me, Josh. I'm longing for you. It's been so long. I want it to be like it was before.'

'No, Kate, don't start.' He turned his head away as she desperately sought his lips. Then he thrust her away, at arm's length. 'I said it's over, Kate.'

'Why?' she cried. 'Why do you hate me?'

'I don't hate you, Kate. But I don't love you, neither. I don't want another man's wife. I got principles. It ain't right.'

'Principles!' she scoffed. 'You didn't have principles six months ago when you took advantage of me.'

'I didn't? Well, maybe I did. It was a two-way thing, Kate. A crazy thing. I'm sorry, I ain't getting involved in it again.'

'What's the matter, cowboy? You scared of Paco?' It was not often she, or anyone else, called her husband by his Christian name. 'You frightened he might come gunning for you? Is it true what he says, you've turned yellow? Gave your herd away?'

'It's over,' he said, thrusting her away. 'He's your man. You've made your bed, you've gotta lie in it.'

'I'll leave him. We'll go away together, Josh.' She held on to him, frantically. 'I'll never give you up. I'm sorry, darling. I've made you angry.'

'Who's thar?' Randy mumbled from the hayloft, raising himself on one elbow, grabbing his gun. 'Is that you, Josh?'

'Is that you, Josh?' she mimicked. 'Oh, go to hell, both of you.'

Logan watched her hurry away down the street and was half-impelled to follow. But he knew that was what she wanted.

'What's wrong?' Randy called.

'Nuthin',' he muttered, still watching her

body moving with a feline grace. 'Nuthin' at all.' He climbed up to the loft, hauled off his boots, stretched out on his soogans a few feet away. 'I wanna make an early start with the stage in the morning. The sooner we git outa this town the better.'

FIVE

John Dog Crandal was feeling mighty pleased with himself as he rode at the head of his bunch. They loped along following the Pecos south. Any man would feel pleased with $2,000 in greenbacks stuffed in his jacket pockets. 'We're gonna paint Fort Sumner red, boys,' he yelled. 'We're gonna live like kings.'

'Yee-hah!' The lanky Luke Clay, who cantered beside him, gave a wild whoop of glee. 'You durn tootin', John Dog. All I want is a bucket of whiskey and three purty gals in bed with me.'

'Three? I'm gonna have me a dozen of them flouncy frails every which-a-way. They won't know what hit 'em. I was born in a tornado,' Crandal whooped. 'That's the way I am.'

Instead of trying to sell the longhorns in Fort Sumner they had herded them up to the railroad town of Las Vegas and got a good price, twelve dollars a head. They hadn't even had to bother changing the Leaning Ladder brand. Just said they were theirs. No more questions asked.

John Dog had paid his men $200 each. That kept them happy. The mares and foals had fetched a pretty price, too. Why reveal that he had pocketed the $2,000? He was the brains of the outfit, wasn't he?

The black stallion had taken some taming, but Crandal's vicious spurs and knotted quirt soon made him see sense.

'Yeah, you bastard,' he snarled, as the beast pranced along beneath him and he kept a firm hold. 'You just try any tricks and I'll rake your ribs 'til the blood flows.'

But John Dog knew better than to beat all spirit out of the stallion. Although Satan tossed his head and chafed at the cruel bit, he sensed the man's domination, and that was the way the man liked it to be.

The same applied to Crandal's domination of men, too. They had to be kept
scared of you. Long gone were the days
when he had been the pariah of a frontier
town, scoffed at by the other boys for being
the bastard of a whore. He had learned the
only way to get respect was to fight, gouge,
kick, knife, to best them with fists and guns.
He had naturally drifted into nefarious
company until soon he was running his own
bunch.

In Texas, before the Rangers made it too
hot for him, he had had no hesitation in killing anyone who stood in his way. But here in
New Mexico he had, he prided himself,
learned more guile. If he could get what he
wanted by threat, by promise of terror, it
would be best. He didn't want the author-
ities on their tail. He had instructed his men
there would be no more murders. Not just
for fun. Not unless it was necessary. Yes, no
wonder he felt on top of the world!

A dozen girls in black stockings, calico

drawers, embroidered bodices, and little else but bangles and beads, stuck their painted faces through the canvas cover of their wagon and screeched like Comanches as Peg Leg Fanny rattled into Fort Sumner and hauled on the reins of the two horses. 'Howdy, boys,' she yelled. 'Here we are! Come and git us!'

Peg Leg Fanny had shut up shop in Stinking Springs as most of the cowboys had ridden back to their ranches for a big round-up. She had decided to try her luck back in this notorious outpost of outlaws. 'Come on, gals,' she yelled, as she unharnessed the nags and let them drink at the big water tank in the centre of the former parade ground. 'Git ya butts down here an' git organized.'

More modestly attired Mexican women were kneeling, washing clothes at the well. They gawped with awe at the new arrivals, these wild, wanton, white women, who were seemingly prepared to sell their bodies and souls to perdition for handfuls of silver.

The Mexicans, with their families, like a few other more law-abiding Americans, had moved into the adobe barracks, officers' quarters, cookhouse, armoury, stables and so forth which had been left vacant inside the fort's crumbling walls.

Peg Leg soon found a spare hut, conveniently close to Beaver Jones's saloon, and quickly moved in her cots and bedding, slinging up a curtain to provide space on the other side for her battered roulette table. A makeshift bar of planks on empty barrels was soon improvized, and she had the girls roll in barrels of her own home-brewed corn liquor. 'Hurry it up, Pearl,' she snapped. 'Get them bottles set up. We ain't come here to stand gossiping.'

She went outside and called to a couple of Mexicans sitting in the shade under their sombreros. 'Hey, you dagos! Any of you handy with a gee-tar? I need musicians.'

It so happened that Peg Leg's wandering red-light district had arrived at the same time as John Dog Crandal's score of *bandidos* galloped in from Las Vegas, money to burn in their pockets and whooping like coyotes when they saw the girls. Soon Fanny's new joint had become a veritable orgy of drunken men, screaming girls, and thrashing limbs behind the curtain.

Fanny had never been so busy; in between snatching two dollars a time for the favours of her calico queens from these evil, lusty *hombres,* she was kept busy filling bottles with coffin varnish to pass across to eager hands. She stood, wiping sweat from her brow and stuffing greenbacks into her capacious underwear. 'What you hanging about fer?' she snarled at Pearl. 'Tell the gals it's shorter-than-short times. We're gonna make a fortune tonight. I'm putting my prices up.'

The wildest, horniest, and thirstiest of the sweaty bunch was some black-haired galoot who had stripped off his buckskin coat to reveal a magnificent physique, a gold necklace around his muscled throat. He was tossing dollars about like confetti, and seemed to have an unending thirst for women and whiskey.

Peg Leg kept her shotgun handy under the

69

counter. She didn't like the look of that razor-sharp machete hanging on his belt. Things might easily turn nasty. But suddenly John Dog was hit by the hard liquor. One moment he was standing tall, a cigar stuck between his gleaming gold teeth, a bottle in his hand, the next he was passed out flat on his face.

'Sling him out,' Peg Leg Fanny roared. 'He's had his fun. Come on, what's it to be, boys?'

While young, slatternly Pearl frantically served the shouting men, Fanny found Crandal's coat, secretively slipped a good portion of the greenbacks that she found in its pockets into her own, then went outside and tossed it on his semiconscious form. She hurried back to get the roulette wheel spinning. 'That bitch, Dawn,' she snarled, cursing the croupier girl. 'She picked a fine time to quit on me.'

'Yee-hagh!' Josh Logan cracked his bullwhip over the backs of the six-horse team the next morning and set the stagecoach, overloaded with passengers, swaying out of White Oaks along the rough, rutted trail. 'First stop Lincoln.'

Due to the fact that the service had been suspended there had been a queue of folks waiting to board so they had six crammed inside and four more on top. The passengers included miners who had made their pile and were heading back East, a farmer's wife in a poke bonnet cackling like the chicken under her arm, a preacher-man in sober garb and black hat and a rouged and beribboned lady of the night. In other words, a mixed bunch.

Kate had planned to travel back with them as far as Roswell but when she saw the company she would have to keep she quickly changed her mind. That was a relief to the Texan. She had insisted on presenting him with a pink-and-purple polka-dot bandanna and a pair of tanned leather gloves. He could hardly refuse. Still, the scarf would be handy keeping the dust out of his throat.

'So long, Josh,' she called, blowing him a kiss as they pulled out. 'Hurry back. I'll be waiting for you.'

He had given her a grudging grin and a wave as he gathered the reins in his new gloves and pulled out. 'She ain't gonna give up on me,' he said. 'She's a lady who likes to git her own way.'

'Why worry?' Randy hooted, clutching his Greener across his chest. 'Love 'em and leave 'em, that was allus my motto.'

'Yeah, sometimes it ain't as easy as that.'

The woman with the chicken hopped off at Lincoln, as well as a couple of other farmers, but they were replaced by a Mexican, his fat wife and two brats.

'Pulling out in half an hour, folks, after we've changed hosses,' Randy shouted as he headed for Rosie's saloon to wet his whistle. 'Don't be late, 'cause we cain't wait. Strict schedule to keep.'

'See you in a minute,' Logan called. 'Git me a beer.'

He stepped into the gun shop and studied

several weapons on the rack. He chose a large-frame, slide-action Thunderer. 'How much?'

'Seventy-five dollars to you, my friend. You know that takes the largest calibre cartridge there is?'

'Yep. Gimme two dozen.'

The owner slid over two boxes of .50-.95s. 'Going hunting?'

'You could say.' Josh grabbed the heavy rifle and joined Randy at the saloon. 'I been spending some of Quinn's expenses cash. We may need extra protection. It's a valuable strongbox we're carrying. There's one of our passengers I don't much like the look of.'

'That shifty-eyed gallows-bird with the scar on his cheek? Aw, don't worry. I'll keep my eye on him.'

'Yeah, well, I don't much like him sitting behind me breathing down my neck.'

There were so many hard-looking characters around it was difficult to judge whom to be most wary of. This one was obviously toting iron beneath the ragged macinaw he wore. But, all men carried guns in these parts. He had, that moment, clattered into the bar, the floorboards thundering under his heavy, spurred boots. He ordered whiskey and ignored them. 'Bit of a mystery, ain't he?' Randy muttered.

It had taken them three hours to get to Lincoln, bouncing up and down on the rough wagon road. Now, high noon, the sun was baking down. Next change of horses would be at Roswell about five in the afternoon. It would be easier once they got to the flatlands of the Pecos valley. But they then had a 170-mile drive before them to reach Las Vegas in the north.

Logan lowered his voice. 'I'm gonna by-pass Fort Sumner. Too many lowlifes hang around there for my liking. We'll head right on to Puerto de Luna. We'll get a change of horses at Conejos Springs. With any luck.'

'That's a hell of a long haul without a break.'

'Yep. Don't worry, pard. We can do it.'

'Time to go.' Randy checked his tin watch. 'All aboard, folks.'

The sun was getting low in the sky by the time they'd covered the fifty miles to Roswell. But it wouldn't get dark until about nine and they'd be well on their way by then. The hard character jumped down when he heard they were bypassing Fort Sumner. 'I'm gonna buy myself a bronc,' he said. 'You're too damn slow for me.'

'Good riddance,' Randy commented, as they watched the *hombre* ride out.

'I ain't so sure,' Josh replied.

They helped sort out a new team and headed for the cantina. The nearby stream was teeming with fish and three fried trout each in their bellies and a pile of black-eye beans made them feel like new men. Logan dunked his head in a horse trough and shouted, 'Let's go, lady and gents. We ain't got no time to lose.'

The Mexican family had descended, too, at Roswell, so they were lighter as they went wheeling out, taking a dusty trail across the waving yellow grasses of the plain. 'It ain't such a bad life,' Randy sang out, enjoying the wind breezing through his bandanna and admiring the way the sun streaked the clouds crimson.

'Yep. You could say.'

Ephraim 'Scarface' Entwistle came charging into Conejos Springs on his new bronco. 'Am I glad to see you here,' he shouted, slithering out of the saddle. 'Thought I'd have to ride up to Sumner to find you. I got great news.'

A scrawny youth in a silk plug hat and a worn overcoat was perched on the corral bar of the staging station. 'I'm here, there an' everywhere these days, Ephraim,' he called. 'I slip into Sumner and out again. It ain't safe to rest no place long. So, what you found out? Spill it.'

'There's five thousand dollars in gold bullion comin' our way, just waitin' to be grabbed.' Scarface smirked proudly. 'Quinn's stage. It'll be along in half an hour or so.'

'Who's driving?' Charley Billings was a hard frontiersman in range leathers. He snorted baccy smoke through his fierce-nostrilled nose. 'Anyone we know?'

'Ain't never seen 'em afore. Jest a coupla deadbeats Quinn's raked up. A tall guy and some old-timer. Won't pose no problem.'

'Five thousand dollars?' Tom Pickles, a former young lawman gone outlaw, gave a whistle of awe. 'That's a thousand each.'

The third man was shaggy, stocky, with a balloon of a beergut. 'Ugly Dave' Richards was wanted for a string of cowardly rapes, stage and train robberies, and killings. He looked what he was: dyed-in-the-wool evil. 'Howja git this info?' he growled.

'A mining office guy got drunk in the Golden Garter, shootin' his mouth off. Doncha worry, it's true. The tall one's got the strongbox under his seat. He's carrying a Thunderer. T'other's got a Greener. Them two's mighty edgy, that's fer sure.'

'That don't sound good.' The young one, Seth Smith, scratched at a red rash of acne on his face. 'What you say, boys?'

'Aw, come on,' Scarface urged. 'It's a godsend. We can head down to old Mexico, have a helluva time with gold like that in our saddle-bags.'

'True. I sure am tired of gettin' hunted from pillar to post, rustlin' a few of Chisum's lousy cows fer a handout.' Seth jumped down from the fence and unhitched his horse. 'Five against two. Not an offer we can rightly refuse.'

'Yeah,' Scarface insisted. 'We can easy take 'em when they pull in here.'

'No, we'll go on ahead, hide out up by Coyote Rocks. We'll take 'em by surprise with the settin' sun at our backs.'

'Good thinking, Seth.' Charley Billings worked at the Yerby ranch, off and on, but thieving was his prime occupation. 'Anybody else on board likely to give us trouble?'

'Nope,' Scarface said. 'There's just some old hoo-er, a coupla miners, an' a preacher-man. We can have what they got, too. Let's move, shall we? They'll be here soon.'

Seth sprang on to his mustang and cantered over to Vittorio Alvaro, who manned the station. 'We'd appreciate it if you don't mention seein' us, Vittorio.' He flicked him a silver dollar. 'OK?'

'*Sí,* you can trust me, *amigo. Adios.*'

The Mexican watched them go until they were just a spiral of dust on the northern plain. Then he heard Randy giving a fanfare on his battered trumpet and turned to see a stagecoach coming in from the south.

Logan wheeled in in a cloud of dust, hauled up and hitched the reins. 'Howdy,' he said, climbing wearily from the box. 'You got a change of horses for us?'

'Ah, *señor.*' Vittorio stroked the grey stubble of his jaw. 'I have horses but Señor Quinn has not paid me. He owe me seexty dollar.'

'Sixty? You don't say? OK.' The Texan dug out his billfold and peeled off the greenbacks. 'Seen anybody around?'

'No, *señor.* Nobody.' He hastily helped

Randy unharness the sweat-streaming team. 'Not a soul in days.'

'Yeah?' Logan picked up a cigar stogie that had been stubbed out on top of a corral post. He sniffed at it. Freshly smoked. His keen eye noticed hoofmarks leading away across the grass. Fresh ones, too. 'You sure about that?'

'Ah, *sí*.' The Mexican saw his disbelief. 'Just a handful of cowboys from the Chisum spread passing by, thass all.'

'Ain't got time to hang around, folks,' Logan shouted, when the new team were in the traces. 'We're rarin' to go.'

'I don't like it,' he gritted out to Randy as they cantered the horses along at a steady jog, leaving Vittorio Alvaro's lonesome outpost far behind. 'Why should he lie? I got a funny feelin' down my spine. Keep that Greener cocked, old-timer.'

SIX

They came out of the blood-red sunset from behind a stark butte, dark silhouettes charging towards them like five horsemen of the Apocalypse.

'I ain't stopping for 'em, if that's what they think,' Logan shouted, snapping the rawhide snake across the horses' backs, sending them into a pounding gallop, their ears flattened back.

He could hear the cracking of revolvers as they drew near. *Tzit!* A bullet ripped through the sleeve of his shirt. The horsemen were riding in line, trying to cut the stagecoach off, bring it to a halt.

He glimpsed a vivid rash on a youngster's face as he cut across on his mustang, tried to grab hold of the leader's head-harness, slow him down. Logan leaned forward sending the sixteen-foot whip cracking again. It snapped around Seth Smith's wrist, sending his revolver spinning in the dust.

'Ouch!' he cried out, like some boy who'd been caned, and fell back, shaking his smarting hand.

Randy fired the Greener and the slug whistled out, hitting Tom Pickles in the shoulder, spinning him from his saddle. Amid a hail of bullets from the other three the coach went charging through and on up the trail.

It was a wild, hectic chase for half a mile or so. Luckily they reached a slight downward gradient and could get up full speed as Logan sent his whip whistling over the terrified team's heads and Randy hung on, looking back, reloading the single-shot Greener. The gunmen had fallen back, but had got over their surprise, and were charging after them, shortening the distance between them as they quirted their mustangs.

'They ain't gonna give up,' Randy shouted, as he took aim and fired, but he was being bounced about so much the shot went wide.

'We'll see about that,' Logan gritted out, hauling on his left-hand rein to pull the horses in a groaning semicircle off the trail and on to the prairie. When they hit an ant-hill he thought for seconds that they would overturn. But the Concord was back on its four sturdy wheels and he was pulling it to a halt. 'Time to take a stand,' he shouted. 'Stay inside, folks.'

He scrambled back to lie flat, Randy beside him, resting their rifles on a box of peaches due to be delivered to Las Vegas. 'Take aim, pardner. Here they come. Let 'em have it.'

The gunmen were grimly charging towards them. Logan's first shot took off Ugly Dave's hat. Randy's sent Charley Billings's mount tumbling and kicking, blood fountaining from its chest.

Boom! Logan's powerful Thunderer rever-berated again, and the heavy slug removed Ephraim 'Scarface' Entwistle's head from his shoulders, brains and bone flying away in a stream of scarlet. His headless body rode on until it eventually tumbled from the saddle.

Seth, bringing up the rear, suddenly had second thoughts about this operation and leapt for cover, cowering in the grass as his mustang shied riderless away.

The youth fired a rapid volley from his Winchester carbine, but at seventy yards range he could not do much damage to the men on top of the coach. 'Jeez!' he cried, as another whistling sizzler from Logan's Thunderer ploughed into the ground and showered him with earth. 'They've turned the damn tables on us. That's for sure.'

To make matters worse, the sun was now in Seth's eyes, and the two miners were leaning from the stage, pistols in their hands, blamming away at him. One however, got too cocky, jumping from the coach to get a better look at the outlaws. Little did he know he was signing his own death warrant. The last slug from Seth's Winchester hit the man right between the eyes.

Charley Billings was down in the grass, too, hiding behind his dead horse, grimly firing at the two on top of the coach, whom he could barely see. One of his slugs ploughed through peaches and splattered Logan with a face full of fruit. At first, Josh thought it was Randy's flesh. But no, it was sweet and tasty.

Like the bullying braggart he was, Ugly Dave was the first to turn tail. He never liked a taste of his own medicine. He quirted his horse away as fast as its hoofs would go.

'Look at 'em run,' Logan yelled, the excitement of battle coursing through his veins.

'Yeah, the lousy polecats,' Randy hollered, sending another bullet whistling past Seth, who had followed Richards's example and was chasing his own runaway mustang across the prairie. 'We sure showed 'em.'

'We sure did, pal.'

Billings was made of sterner stuff, but even he was unmanned by their onslaught, and by the memory of the headless horseman galloping past him. He jumped up from behind his dead horse and ran off after Seth, desperate to get out of range.

When Seth caught his mount he cantered back to Billings and hoisted him up behind him.

'Who were those guys?' Charley asked.

'I seen 'em afore,' Seth mused. 'Used to drive for Quinn up to six months ago. Had some sorta fallin' out. Never seen 'em in action before. You gotta give it to them. They sure can handle 'emselves.'

Tom Pickles was sitting peering at the bloody hole through his shoulder. Tears coursed down his cheeks as he moaned, 'I'm dyin', boys. I'm done fer.'

'Aw, quit whinin',' Richards growled. 'It's only a damn flesh wound. Slug's gawn straight through. Get on your hoss. If you ain't with us by the time we reach Fort Sumner we'll assume you musta dropped off dead.'

They set off trailing disconsolately towards the old fort, while back at the coach the hysterical 'painted lady' was being revived with smelling-salts. She got hysterical again when they hauled the dead miner in to sit beside her.

Randy led the men over to peer at the headless Entwistle. 'Aren't you going to bury him?' the Bible-thumper quavered.

'You jokin'?' Randy spat on the corpse. 'Coyote gotta eat, ain't they?'

The preacher made the sign of the cross. 'At least he's freed of his earthly troubles.'

'Yeah.' Logan patted the trusty Thunderer. 'You could say we sent him to happy oblivion. But I ain't sure what the Good Lord will make of him.'

'He sure looks better dead than he did alive,' Randy chuckled. 'I never did take to that feller.'

It was past midnight by the time the exhausted team had covered another thirty-five miles and rattled the stage into Puerto de Luna. But there was a lamp still burning in the cantina and store of the former priest, Padre 'Polaco'.

Polish by birth, his true name was Alexander Grzelachowski, but the local Latinos couldn't get their tongues around that. 'What's happened?' he cried, as they dragged the dead miner in. Randy, the lady, the other miner, all began babbling at once about the attack.

'It must have been Seth Smith, him and that scum he rides with,' the Pole conjectured. 'You say a buck-toothed scrawny youth in a Lincoln top hat with a rash across his face? That's him. He used to pretend he was my friend, then stole my horses behind my back.'

'You can't trust that li'l weasel an inch,' a gruff voice butted in. 'He's only nineteen but musta killed half a dozen men. Kills without provocation, without reason. Mind you, he's fast.'

The owner of the voice was Whiskey Jim Greathouse, a big man made taller by his white Stetson. He was seated in a corner of the cantina with his sidekick, named Brad. That accounted for the wagon loaded with barrels outside, which they were probably hauling from Las Vegas to White Oaks.

Logan had heard that he was a man renowned for selling whiskey to the Indians and was generally a dark operator, so he merely grunted a reply. 'Yeah? You think so?'

When a Mexican ostler had been roused to go change the horses, rub them down and water them, Logan, Randy and the passengers from the stage sat down to plates of boiled beef and chillied beans.

'The same old thang,' Randy groaned, 'but it sure tastes good tonight. There were moments back there when I thought it was goodbye. Them were tight papers, that's fer sure. Reminds me of that time the Messys attacked us at Shirt Tail Crossing...'

'What you got to drink?' Logan asked.

'Whiskey,' Polaco said. 'Jim's just delivered me three barrels.'

Randy guffawed. 'We ain't plannin' on drinkin' that much.'

'Whiskey's the stuff to put lead in your pencil,' Jim said with a laugh. 'Seein' as you're such brave boys and saved the lady's life, I bet she could be mighty grateful.'

The painted sinner in her rustling skirts fluttered her eyelashes. 'We'll have to see about that when we get to Vegas.'

But she suddenly screamed as an eight-inch centipede dropped from the ceiling into her soup and splashed about wiggling its toxic mandibles. Logan scooped it out with a spoon and flicked it through the open door. 'All adds to the flavour, ma'am.'

'She'll be more'n grateful now,' Whiskey Jim growled. 'You might even git it cut price.'

'We'll drink to that.' Logan took a swig from the bottle by the neck. 'Yeah, that's better.'

'So, you're Quinn's new driver, are ya?' Brad McNulty, the hunky young assistant to Whiskey Jim asked. 'Kinda stepped into my shoes?'

'Why, are *you* the one who jacked it in?'

'Too true. I couldn't stand the pace. I guess you know what kinda pace I'm speakin' of? The attentions of a certain lady.'

'Kate?' The word came out involuntarily, such was Logan's surprise. 'You mean you ... she?'

'Whew? That woman's insatiable, ain't she? A reg'lar meat-mincer.'

Logan frowned, and took another swig of the throat-rasping liquor. 'I don't know what you're talking about.'

'So, it's true.' Jim laughed. 'I'd heard rumours to that effect, that Kate likes to keep herself a handsome stud on the side.' He slapped Logan's knee. 'Come on, mister. Don't play coy.'

'She's sure some gal,' Brad said. 'But it ain't all clover. Somcone tittle-tattled to Quinn. That's why I got out, 'fore he came gunnin' for me.'

Logan got to his feet. 'I'd ask you to shut your mouth about this, you blabbermouth. It ain't gentlemanly.' He eased the Light-ning on his hip. 'The Quinns are friends of mine.'

'Aw, no need to git riled up,' the young

man protested. 'I'm only telling it like it is. You'll find out.'

Logan turned on his heel. 'Come on, folks. Ain't got time to hang around. We got fresh horses and we're ready to go.'

He spotted a shovel in a corner and tossed it hard at the lover boy. 'Here, if you got so much energy, maybe you could bury the stiff?' He flipped a quarter at him contemptuously. 'That should cover it.'

SEVEN

The walls of Fort Sumner glowed a ruddy red as the rays of the rising sun flickered in the east. John Dog Crandal groaned as he stirred, flat on his face in the dust. He sat up and looked around. He wasn't the only one. Several of his *companeros* lay where they had fallen, thrown from Peg Leg Fanny's whorehouse. They had snored away the night in drunken stupor.

The gaunt and lanky Luke Clay came to his senses at the same time. 'Gawd, my guts,' he moaned. 'There's a gang of snakes writhing in my belly. What's she put in that stuff?'

Crandal retrieved his stained buckskin jacket. 'I feel like I've been run over by an elephant,' he said. In fact, in the darkness men had stamped their boots on his prostrate form as they went in and out of the brothel. Some might have urinated on him, judging by the sticky smell of his coat.

'Shee-it! What's happened to me cash?' he asked, searching the coat pockets. 'I couldn't have spent all that.'

Of the $1,000 in greenbacks that had been in his pocket all he had left was a measly fifty or so dollars and a handful of cents. 'I've been damn well robbed.'

'So?' Luke grinned. 'The way you were whoopin' it up, whatja expect?'

John Dog's band had made camp underneath the nearby wall and were brewing up coffee. He went across, helped himself to a tin mug of the scalding brew, and checked his saddle-bags. At least, the other $1,000 was still intact.

He found his faded pink vest and pulled it on for he had got cold lying out half-naked all night. He checked his big Remington revolver, stuffed it into his belt and strode across to Peg Leg Fanny's hut. He grabbed her by the neck of her flannel nightdress and dragged her from her cot. 'Where's my cash, you thievin' haybag?' He slapped her. 'Give it back you, lousy witch.'

Fanny shrieked like a banshee, rousing the girls, who came from behind the suspended sheet looking like they'd crawled through a hedge backwards. They scrambled, screaming and grabbing hold of John Dog.

'All we've got is what you owed us,' Pearl whined, loyally protecting her mistress as he beat them off. 'You practic'ly drank the place dry.'

Crandal backed off. 'Listen, you harpies,' he screeched. 'Nobody could have spent that much.'

'Now you mention it,' Peg Leg said,' I did notice four fellers ride in late. One was stooped over you, rifling your pockets, that's who it was.'

'Who was he?' John Dog demanded.

'A skinny young sonuvagun in a plug hat. Looked to me like that Seth Smith.'

'Who's he?' Crandal asked.

'Aw, some no-good rustler. Comes and

goes like most of you.' Fanny hitched up her nightie to adjust her peg leg. 'Fancy attacking a poor lady like this. I've a good mind to report you to the sheriff.'

'Arr, shut up. Where can I find this Smith?'

'In Beaver's saloon, I guess. Why?' Fanny taunted. 'You gonna call him out?'

'I wouldn't, if I were you.' Pearl gave a wide-eyed, fearful look. 'He's some gun-slinger.'

'Get stuffed, you bitches.' John Dog turned on his heel and went back to his men.

'I got a job for you, Luke,' he said. 'I need somebody killed.'

'Sure.' Luke Clay grinned. 'I ain't killed nobody since we left Texas. You said not to.'

'Yeah, well, I've changed my mind. We'll go halves on whatever's in his pockets. OK?'

'Who is he?'

'Just some gutter trash called Smith. Don't worry. He's nobody special. We'll back you if there's trouble.'

It was about noon when Seth in his stove

pipe hat and worn brocade vest, strolled into Beaver's saloon followed by Charley, Ugly Dave and the shoulder-bandaged Tom Pickles.

'That's him,' Crandal muttered. 'That spotty-faced li'l creep.'

He, and about fifteen of his *viciosos* were sprawled on one side of the saloon, recovering from the excesses of the night before.

'That li'l punk.' The lanky Luke got to his feet. 'He looks about as useless as a flea on a dawg's dick.' Luke had already been hitting the whiskey and, as he stood centre floor, was bristling for a fight, secure in the knowledge that Crandal's gang could blow Smith and his boys to hell.

'Hey, pint-size,' he jeered at Seth, who was seated at a table on the other side of the saloon dealing from a greasy pack of cards. 'Has your mammy let you out to play with the big boys?'

'Somethin' botherin' you, mister?' Seth peered at Luke, then whipped out his Smith & Wesson revolver, whirling it on one finger, before slipping it back into a holster pig-stringed to his thigh. 'If so, spit it out.'

John Dog gave a roar of laughter. 'You don't impress us with those fancy tricks, sonny boy. Maybe you didn't appreciate who you were sneak-thievin' from last night. My name's Crandal, these are my boys, and Luke there's my first lieutenant. He's requested the honour of killin' you.'

'What you talking about?' Seth scratched at his rash that had intensified in colour. 'I ain't no thief.'

'Well, we say you are.' Luke turned to wink at the men to make sure they appreciated his wit. 'I say he must be one of them molly boys, don't you, fellas? That's where he picked up that rash – from selling his backside.'

'Don't push it, pal,' Charley snarled, stroking his jaw, staring hard.

'Yeah? What's the li'l darlin' gonna do about it?' Luke sauntered, unsteadily, across to Seth's table. 'So, mammy lets you play cards, does she?'

Seth looked up, apprehensively, but deftly dealt the deck. 'You're making a mistake, friend,' he said.

'Listen to him.' Luke lurched back to his own side and took another swig from the whiskey bottle. 'You ever seen such a miserable li'l shit?'

While his back was turned Seth eased out the Smith & Wesson and moved the cylinder forward three notches. When fired the hammer would now hit three spent cases that he hadn't removed. 'What's your handle, feller?' he called.

'Luke Clay. You better remember it.' Clay spun around, his hand covering his own six-gun. 'You better hand back that money you stole.'

Charley looked across uneasily at the grinning gang of badmen. He didn't like the look of them or the odds. 'He's calling you out, Seth. What you gonna do?'

'You're on your own,' Ugly Dave growled. 'This ain't nuthin' to do with me.'

Seth stood and smiled nervously. 'Seems

like I got an advantage over you, Luke. It wouldn't be fair. This is a hundred-dollar piece.' He offered it by its barrel for inspection. 'It's deadly accurate. Not like that worn-out ol' Colt of yourn. But, even if we swapped guns, I figure I could still beat you.'

'Yeah?' Luke, surprised, grinned. 'You think? Right!' He grabbed the Smith & Wesson and handed his own Colt across. 'Let's just see about that.'

'It's up to you, Luke,' John Dog growled, beckoning to his men to keep out of it. 'You sure you can take him now?'

'Yeah.' Clay suddenly had the look of a furtive ferret, but it was too late to back down. He examined the revolver. 'Nice piece. Don't need cocking, do it? Let's go for it.'

Seth called out, 'Thirty paces, OK?' He turned his back on Luke and paced towards the door. 'I'll take my stand over here.'

Mad-eyed, Clay didn't wait for him to turn, aiming the fancy shooter, hastily squeezing the trigger. Once, twice, three times the hammer clicked and nothing occurred. 'Shee-it!'

100

Seth didn't wait for him to try a fourth. He spun around, took careful aim and the old Colt crashed out. Once, twice, three times, too.

Clay went flying backwards and hit the bar, sliding to a sitting position, glassy-eyed. Blood pumped from three holes in his shirt. Seth tossed the Colt away and went to retrieve his own revolver. 'Sorry, Luke. I was just too clever for you. You should beware taking gifts from a stranger.'

John Dog stared, bemused. 'What a crafty li'l mutha! Maybe you and me should join forces. Between us we could carve up this territory.'

Seth grinned as he returned to his card game. 'I'll think about it,' he sang out.

Mandolins, guitars, drums and trumpets rang out in a pounding, raucous chorus as the Mexican population at Fort Sumner enjoyed a *bailie* in one of the old barrack halls. Cotton-clad men shrilled their voices in harmony as laughter and curses rang like silver pesos.

One of the dandiest dancers on the floor was young Seth Smith, who had ingratiated himself with the Mexican sheepherders as a way of getting to know their daughters.

His partner and sweetheart that night was Paulita Jennings, a mixed-race girl. Like many settlers in these parts her father, Jack Jennings, a storekeeper, had taken a Mexican wife.

The buck-toothed Seth could afford to be merry in spite of the setback of the aborted stage robbery. He had spent the day playing poker with whiskey-soaked John Dog and had fleeced him of a good many dollars.

'I do not like that John Dog and his *bandidos,*' Paulita said, as they took a break from the dancing outside under the stars. 'They are not the sort we want here.'

'Aw, he's OK,' Seth grinned. 'Just a tad crazy. He's got this idea about running some sort of protection scheme. He wants me to join him. I told him gamblin's more my scene. He's gone off in a huff, says he's gonna put the screws on Quinn.'

When the army had moved out of the fort about thirty Latino families had moved in, mostly running herds of sheep in the hills. The Spanish-speaking Seth was popular as he spread his ill-gotten gains around in return for safe-hiding at their camps. But neither the Latinos nor the white settlers had expected the fort to become the stomping ground of so much riff-raff.

'Hey,' Seth whispered to Paulita, tickling her ear. 'How about you sneak me into your room? I gotta ride out in the morning.'

'You *are* going to marry me, aren't you, Seth?' the girl murmured, as she unglued her lips from his. 'We *will* go to live in Mexico, like you said?'

'True, we'll settle down there and have lots of little ones. I sure am tired of running.'

'How many other girls have you said that to?'

Seth grinned, for he had said it to quite a few in order to get his wicked way. 'It's you I love best,' he sang out, putting an arm around her waist and swinging her across the former parade ground towards the Jennings's store. 'Believe me, honey, that's the truth.'

It was a warm summer's night, the stars and moon glowed in the heavens above, and Pauilita was easily convinced.

'I'm getting some cash put by,' Seth said. 'Jest need a lucky break. Don't worry, darlin'. We'll head for the border purty soon.'

'When I heard those shots coming from the saloon today my heart was in my mouth. I just knew it was you,' the girl said. 'You worry me, Seth. Won't the sheriff come after you?'

'Nah. Why should he. I'm doin' his job for him. If anyone deserved killin' it was that Luke Clay. I feel real good tonight for putting that dog down. Nobody's gonna put me in the hoosegow,' the youth boasted. 'I'm a boy who'll allus ride free.'

EIGHT

Josh Logan and Randy had not lingered long amid the railyards, hotels and saloons of bustling Las Vegas. Long enough to hand over the strongbox of bullion to two Wells Fargo guards in the armoured caboose of a locomotive headed back East to New York. A banker's draft would be paid into Quinn's account for the gold.

'That guy jest cain't lose,' Randy opined. 'He'll be a millionaire in a year or two.'

'Yep,' Logan half-agreed, 'if his luck holds out.'

He headed the crowded stage back down the Pecos, the six-horse team eating up the miles through Villa Nueva, Anton Chico, Santa Rosa, Puerto de Luna, until they rolled into Fort Sumner.

'Just a short stay, folks,' Logan sang out.

'We'll be on our way again in an hour.'

That was if there was no trouble. Logan was on edge at the possibility of running into John Dog Crandal and his villainous crew, or the youthful Seth Smith and the gang who had attacked the coach. What could he do against such men except face them down? He loosened the Colt Lightning in its holster as he stepped warily into Beaver's saloon.

But it seemed the birds had flown. So it was not without a sense of relief that he slapped the white dust from his clothes and downed a beer and a dish of tripe.

Before leaving, he checked his .38. It was Colt's first double-action that had come out in '76. He had sent fifteen dollars for it, mail order, when he read an advertisement saying, 'This pistol exceeds in accuracy and penetration any other of its class.' However, any man who used it would need to be good to beat, in close combat, John Dog or his professional killers. And Smith was said to be fast.

'Can you take the mail pouch along to Pete Maxwell's?' he asked Randy. 'I'm gonna call in on Peg Leg Fanny. Seems she's moved in along the street.'

'Oh, yeah,' Randy guffawed. 'Still got that li'l piece of muslin on your mind?'

'Maybe.' First, he cooled off over at the tank, combing back his long flaxen hair. Yes, it was true, he had Dawn Adamson on his mind. Funny, the thought of seeing her made his heart thump more than the prospect of bumping into Crandal.

'Howdy,' he called, as he entered the brothel. 'How's it going?'

Half-dressed, the girls were sitting idly around, and Fanny was stocking the bar. 'Well, if it ain't the handsome stranger. You lookin' fer a good time?'

'I ... er...' He glanced around. 'Is that croupier girl, Dawn, here?'

'No, she damn well ain't. She lit out.'

'Why so?' He lit a cheroot and paid for drinks all round.

'Because all she wanted to do was be a

croupier. To put it frankly, mister, she refused to go horizontal with the customers. What makes her think herself so precious? Snooty li'l cow. You don't open your legs, I tol' her, you can hightail it. Thass what she done. Went off with my banjo man, the coloured boy.'

'Where to?'

'Who cares? Why you worryin'? There's plenty lovely gals here. Take your pick.'

'Ain't got time. I'm driving stage for Quinn. Gotta be moving out. Got a strict schedule.'

'Yeah, same old story.'

'Any sign of a Fort Worth roughneck called John Dog?'

'Crandal? Don't ask. He was behaving like Casanova gone berserk. Then had the nerve to say I robbed him. He and his boys – minus one who gotten killed – moved out a coupla days ago. Unlike you, my friend, he was no gen'l'man. Me and my girls are still recovering. Plus the fact that them green-backs of his look to me like crude forgeries.'

Logan grinned. 'Yeah, I can guess. So

long, y'all. Take it easy.'

The girls came to the door to wave as he and Randy, with their assorted passengers, moved out of the fort and set the horses cantering across the baking prairie. A hundred miles to go to Roswell.

Kate Quinn sat before her bedroom mirror in Roswell and brushed back her crackling auburn hair as her maid cinched tight her corset. The sun's setting rays filtered through her window as she stepped into a flouncy silk dress, with a plunging front, very *décolletée*. She didn't normally dress so elegantly for dinner with Quinn, but if Josh Logan was keeping to timetable he should be bringing in the stage from Vegas in an hour or so. 'He's gonna git the full treatment,' she murmured, smiling at her image. 'See if he can resist me.'

Suddenly, however, the calm of their oasis in the prairie was rudely broken by the clatter of gunfire and shouting and hooting as if they were under attack by Apaches.

But no. These were no Mescaleros. As she peered out she saw that the house was surrounded by a band of horsemen, Mexicans and white gutter trash, all firing off with abandon the carbines in their hands, bullets whining through windows, smashing vases, ricocheting off the adobe walls.

'What the hell's happening?' she screamed, as Quinn came rushing in.

'Get down,' he yelled. 'Keep outa sight. I'll deal with this.'

But Kate could see the fear in the whites of his eyes. And in a way she couldn't blame him. These killer scum were enough to frighten anybody.

'I'm coming out.' Quinn poked a white shirt tied to a rifle through the bead curtain of the house doorway. 'Don't shoot me.'

The fusillade gradually ceased. John Dog Crandal urged Satan closer and waited expectantly. 'Come out, then.'

Quinn showed himself, holding the rifle to the ground. 'What do you want?'

'Cash.' John Dog gave a throaty laugh and

shouted, 'We know you got plenty of it. We want two thousand dollars in golden eagles. No paper dollars. There are too many forged greenbacks in circulation. Two thousand in gold. Hand it over and we go, leave you in peace.'

'You're crazy.' Quinn uttered the words in his hoarse whiskey voice. 'I don't keep that sorta cash in the house. My money is in the bank at Vegas. Or in my safe at the White Oaks mine.'

Kate suddenly pushed through the doorway beside him, her green eyes flashing with anger. She, too, had a rifle in her hand but hers was aimed at Crandal. 'What are you parleying with these scum of the earth for? Tell them to get off of our property.'

'Get back inside.' Quinn put an arm across her. 'I'll handle this.'

'You!' Kate hissed, scornfully. 'Give them a taste of lead. That's the only talk these devil's spawn understand.'

Crandal shrugged black hair from his face and his lips curled back in a leering grin as

111

he peered at her partly bared bosom, the dipping neckline of her skimpy dress. 'This your wife? Hey, I like what I see.'

Others of his men gave shrill catcalls, making obscene suggestions as they laughed at her.

'Where you find your wife?' John Dog asked. 'In a bordello? Tell you what: I will have the whore in part payment. So then you only owe me one thousand nine hundred dollars in gold. That is a generous offer.'

'I'm not for barter,' Kate shrilled. 'Don't think I am. I spit in the face of a cur like you. You lay a finger on me and you'll have a posse of decent white men in this county after you so fast you won't know what hit you.'

John Dog grinned. 'She's sure got a lot of sass, ain't she, boys? She's just the sorta fancy lady who needs takin' down a peg or two. How about we give her a good–?'

'Look,' Quinn interrupted, pulling out his wallet, thumbing the notes. 'I swear this is all I got here. Two hundred dollars or so. It's yours.' He tossed it to John Dog who deftly caught it in one hand. 'I'll get you the rest in gold. Just give me a few days.'

'We don't want trouble,' John Dog cajoled. 'There is no need for any bloodshed. We will be back in four days. You have our two thousand in gold ready and waiting, OK? Otherwise, I will have that woman in front of your eyes, while my men hold you with a noose round your neck. Then – *boom* – we will blow your house to hell.'

'All right, I'll have it ready here.'

'And don't go blabbing to the army or the sheriff, neither. If I suspect double dealing' – John Dog pointed a finger at Kate – 'she dies.'

He gave a yell, hauled the prancing Satan around, and spurred him away, followed by his men.

Quinn watched them go, his hair over his eyes, his face tense, then he pushed Kate back inside. 'What you dressed up like a two-bit whore for? Cain't you see you've given him ideas? What for you walking around like some half-naked hussy. Where's that whiskey gone?'

When he had found the bottle and filled a glass tumbler with an unsteady hand, tipping it back with a gasp, he stared at her and groaned, 'Ah, I get it. You're expectin' Logan back tonight. You're half-crazy about that guy.'

'Why don't you talk some sense,' Kate replied, laying the rifle aside. 'And go get the sheriff. Tell him we need protection. Why are you so scared of that bunch of ragtails?'

'Admit it!' Quinn caught her by the throat. 'You got eyes for Josh Logan, ain'tcha?' He increased pressure as she struggled like a bird caught in a net and forced her back over a table. 'That's why he left before. It's true, isn't it?' He laughed harshly in her face. 'That's a joke 'cause he don't want you. He's too decent a feller to want a whore like you. See, so you're stuck with me and where you are. You do what I say or–'

'Or what?' she cried defiantly, trying to

make him loosen his grip.

'Or,' Quinn shouted, 'I'll toss you to Crandal and his dogs like the piece of trash that you are.'

'Brave words,' she sneered, as he released her. 'You're afraid of them so you pick on me. What sort of man are you?'

'You behave,' Quinn shouted. 'I can take so much and no more. That's a warning.'

NINE

'What was that shooting?' Randy shouted, as Logan drove the stagecoach on along the white dusty trail that gleamed in the moonlight. 'It sounded like it was coming from Roswell.'

'Keep your Greener primed, old-timer,' Josh gritted out. 'There might be more trouble.'

When he hauled in outside Quinn's place he saw in the lanternlight estate workers scurrying around, throwing out shattered mirrors and vases. 'Looks like they been under siege.'

'Oh, Josh!' Kate Quinn met him at the kitchen door, raising her arms as if she wanted him to hug her to him. 'Why didn't you come sooner? We could have done with a real man around here.'

116

Logan tried to evade her embrace as best he could. 'What's happened?'

'It's John Dog Crandal,' she cried. 'He's been shooting up the place, making horrible threats to me. Disgusting things he said. He wants two thousand dollars. Or me. What can we do?'

'Why are you asking *him*?' Quinn roared, hanging on to the kitchen table, waving the bottle around.

Logan pushed past her as gently as he could and asked Quinn, 'You're not going to pay, are you?'

'My whole life's wrapped up in this place, in the mine, in the stage company. I've got to pay,' Quinn whined. 'What else can I do? That cur Crandal means what he says. Look what he did to you.'

'Look how white Paco's gone. His hand's shaking,' Kate cried. 'What kind of husband is he? You're a wise man, Josh. Tell him what we should do.'

'You shut your mouth,' Quinn shouted. 'What's it to do with him?'

'I would like to ask his opinion, do you mind? He is going to be our partner, after all. I'd like his advice.'

'Some partner,' Quinn snorted. 'A sleepin' partner is what you'd like him to be.'

'My advice would be you all calm down. But if you really want to know, I wouldn't give Crandal a peso. If you pay him now, he'll be back and he'll want double or triple next time.'

'Yeah, that's easy for you to say, pal. It ain't your house he's gonna put to the flames, your woman he's gonna rape.' Quinn held his glass aloft and stared at them both. 'Or is she? Mine?'

'Take no notice of him, Josh,' Kate put in. 'He's drunk. He's talking rot.'

'Yeah, so *you* go fight him.'

'Ach,' she sneered. 'You make me sick.'

'Those sorta words don't help none,' Logan said, moving away from her to help himself to a drink. 'But I figure you gotta fight him, Paco. There ain't nuthin' else you can do.'

'Pah!' Quinn spat out. 'I got a bandit sittin' on my back and what am I surrounded by – a crazy wife and a lousy hero.'

Suddenly, Quinn lurched forward, pushing Logan away. 'Clear off. Get outa my house. You're the lousy snake in the grass. Not Crandal.'

Randy, who had been watering and unharnessing the horses, burst in. 'What's going on? Shall I rig up a new team? Or are we staying here? We've been on that box eighteen hours. I'm just about stoved in.'

'We'll go on to Lincoln,' Logan replied, his face grim. 'I knew we should have never taken on this job again.'

He was in the stables putting the finishing touches to the harness of the fresh horses in the traces when Kate caught hold of him in the semi-darkness. She held him close, pressing her breasts tight to his chest, her face entreating him. 'Josh, take me with you,' she cried. 'I can't stand it here another minute. Take me with you tonight.'

Her perfume was almost overpowering

and he was tempted, he had to admit, to kiss her, to have her one last time. But he firmly placed her aside and swung up on to the box. 'We got a full passenger complement,' he drawled, moving the team out. 'Ain't got room for another.'

The coach loaded, six squashed inside, and four on top, he snaked his whip cracking over the fresh horses' ears and they lumbered away into the night on the fifty-mile climb to Lincoln.

Bounced about inside the coach like a pea in a bucket, Azariah Wilde groaned and peered through the buckskin curtain at the moon-streaked barren crags. How much further would he have to travel through this godforsaken country before his mission was completed?

Wilde was a Pinkerton detective, seconded to the federal secret service. He had been to see the state governor in Santa Fe. A forgery ring had been churning out dud greenbacks. It was believed to be operating out of this area. He would be expected to rake through this rugged terrain seeking their hideout.

It was five in the morning by the time they rolled into Lincoln. Wilde, in his dark suit and derby, climbed stiffly down and called, 'Where's the sheriff's office?'

'Across the road,' Logan said.

'Who's that pasty-faced dude?' Randy asked. 'What's he want?'

'Beats me.' Logan rubbed at his tired eyes. It had been a long trail. There would be no sleep until they reached White Oaks. He banged on the door of Rosie's saloon. 'Breakfast here for half an hour,' he called out to the passengers. 'Then we go the last forty-five miles up through the hills. Don't know about y'all, but I'll be damned glad to get to White Oaks.'

TEN

'Tomorrow we'll raid Chisum's herd,' Seth Smith called out to Charley, Ugly Dave and Tom Pickles as they sprawled around their campfire. 'We need to raise some hard cash.'

'Yeah, we can sell 'em to old Pat Murphy,' Charley hooted. 'He'll give us a good price. Old Pat'll buy anythang. He's no love for Chisum, neither.'

In fact, the Irishman had grabbed some land to ranch further down the valley, on the edge of the cattle baron's empire. He had also built a saloon and hotel for passing travellers. 'Him and Old John are like two hounds with teeth bared,' Charley said.

'I don't like it, Seth. Things aren't going well. The raid on the stage was a disaster.' Tom had been silent all night, laid out in his blanket by the fire, nursing his wounded shoulder. 'I think we should leave Chisum alone, head for the border now while we got the chance.'

'You ain't losing your nerve, are you, Tom?'

Seth grinned. 'We can't head for Mexico stony-broke. I promise you this'll be our last raid, then we'll go.'

Tom's wound had been patched up at the fort by one of the Mexican women, but the bullet hole was raw-edged and pounding painfully. There was an eerie feel about the dark, eroded rocks around this hideout, the flickering firelight, and the lugubrious screeching of owls. 'I just got the feelin' our luck's running out,' he whispered.

'Aw, quit whining,' Ugly Dave retorted. 'Why'd you bring this cowardly whelp along fer, Smith? He ain't no use to us in that state.'

'Tom's my pal,' Seth said, and asked Charley, 'You sure Murphy will pay?'

'Yeah, Pat'll give us eight dollars a head,' Charley said. 'He'll sell 'em to gov'ment contractors for double that. He'll be glad to have 'em. Old Pat's a pretty hard thief. He's stealing every which way he can.'

'Sounds like us, eh, boys?' Seth cried, setting them off laughing. 'Only thang Ol' Pat won't steal's a red-hot stove. We sure ain't gonna git our fingers burned stealing a few old cows.'

They woke at first light and set off down the Pecos valley. After a couple of hours they came across a nice little herd of about 200 beeves in fine fettle. 'These'll do, boys,' Seth shouted. It was an easy matter to round them up and send them skittering.

Or, it would have been. But, suddenly, two of Chisum's cowboys appeared riding fast across the rustling grass towards them. One had a revolver in his fist and fired a warning shot as he approached. 'Hey!' he yelled. 'What you doing with them cattle?'

Seth jerked his mustang around, jacked a shell into his Winchester and hit the cowboy square on, knocking him back off his saddle.

'What you think, dummy?'

The cowboy's companion reined in, gawped down at the body in the grass, then croaked, 'You done killed him.'

'Yeah. You lookin' fer the same treatment?'

As the cowboy jerked his reins with an expression of terror and spurred his mustang away, Seth put a bullet in his back, rolling him into the grass. He cantered across and put another in to make sure. 'Don't do to have witnessess,' he grinned. 'Dead men tell no tales. Ain't that what they say?'

It didn't take long to herd the longhorns at a fast clip towards the Irishman's lonesome hotel on the prairie.

'Jasus, boys,' Murphy roared. 'You ain't even changed the brands on 'em. Never mind, get 'em in the corral, then come and cut the dust from your throats.'

In the bar he poured them all a stiff whiskey and counted out $1,000. 'That's the best I can do for stolen beeves. Now be off widja. It ain't advisable for me to be seen doin' business wid the likes of youse.'

They split the cash and got back on their mustangs. 'See, I told ya it would be OK, Tom,' said Seth. 'You and Dave go back to the hideout. Me an' Charley have business at the fort. We'll see ya in a coupla days, then head for the border.'

'Why you got to go to Sumner for?' Tom called out. 'It ain't safe there. Chisum's gonna be on the warpath.'

'Aw, you worry too much, Tom. Truth is I wanna see Paulita. I gotta say goodbye. Or, who knows, I might even bring her along.'

Tom shook his head as he watched Seth go. 'He's crazy.'

'Yeah,' Ugly Dave muttered, darkly. 'A man's prick has oft been his undoin'.'

ELEVEN

The Four Aces was the best-run gambling den in White Oaks. The curtains were kept drawn night and day and there was no clock on the wall so, unless you consulted your own pocket watch, you had no idea what time it was. Most men were so busy concentrating on their cards they paid time little heed. Sometimes a poker game could go on for three days and nights as the chips piled up. The whale-oil lanterns were kept low and any rowdiness was quickly taken care of by the casino-minders. All the tables, monte, blackjack, keno, would generally be packed and miners stood three deep around the roulette tables, but conversation was subdued unless somebody had a big win and was celebrating. Or a loser had to be thrown out of the joint, protesting vociferously. The miners had gold to burn, but they were greedy for more. Or was it just a compulsion, a heart-thumping, intensified form of risk-taking that made them flock there?

Josh Logan had slept for twelve hours, then soaked in a tub at the bathhouse. After a shave and trim at the barbershop, he bought himself a new wool check shirt and cavalry twill tight pants, and felt like a new man. He handed in his gun as he stepped inside the casino and found a place at the bar.

'Whiskey straight,' he said, and glanced around at the tables, the bearded, scruffy miners, the tradesmen in dark suits, and the nattily attired professional gambling men puffing on cheroots and contemplating their cards.

'Hi.' The slim brunette, Dawn Adamson, slipped on to a bar stool beside him. 'What's your game?'

'Oh, hiya.' She had taken him by surprise, appearing as if out of nowhere. 'What's yours?'

'Blackjack. But I can't do you any favours. Nuthin's rigged here, I'm glad to say.'

'I ain't asking for none. But I guess blackjack'll be my game, too. Not that I'm one of your big spenders. I only got fifty dollars to risk.'

'A gambler ought to know how much he can lose. A pity more don't.' She smiled at him, her cheek dimpling, mischievously. 'If they all did, however, I'd probably be out of a job.'

'No fear of that with this crowd. Fancy a drink?'

'No. I'm just going on duty. I've been asleep upstairs.' She was in a dress of rustling turquoise silk, a little less severe tonight, revealing her pale throat. A gold crucifix on a chain dangled on her chest. 'Maybe, if you're still around at midnight, we could.'

'I'll be here.'

'Just a drink. I ain't promisin' nuthin' else.'

'I wasn't expecting nuthin'. It'd be nice to talk.'

'Just as long as that's understood. There's

so many heavy gropers around.' She grinned at him, showing neat white teeth between her crimson-painted lips. 'You look quite the dude tonight.'

'Yep.' He took a swig of his whiskey and met her eyes. 'Back in Stinking Springs I guess I looked beat up. Which was what I was. We'd had a spot of bother. But I've just drawn what's owed me for taking the stage to Las Vegas and back. So, I'm enjoying a bit of rest and recreation.'

'Which means hitting the hot spots?'

'To tell the truth I was half-hoping you'd be here.'

'That's funny,' she laughed, 'because I'd been rather hoping to see you again.'

'That's good news.' He flicked his hair out of his eyes and asked, 'So how did you get to be a gambling lady?'

'My daddy taught me. What else is a gal to do?'

'I guess it pays well.'

'You get tips. Last night some old galoot was shooting chips at me like bullets from a gun. He couldn't believe he'd spent a thousand dollars when he dropped out. But he was generous. He tucked a fifty-dollar bill in my garter.'

Logan didn't much like the sound of that. But it was the custom. If a gal hoicked up her dress to show a silk-stockinged leg it was much appreciated by some lonesome old miner. He assumed that that was all she had showed.

'Blackjack ain't really my game,' he said, to take his mind off it. 'Kinda complicated.'

'People play a lot of systems. There's a lot of unspoken rules. But usually the most skilled person wins. I'll have to show you sometime. Uhuh, here comes the pit boss. I can't hang around. See you later, perhaps?'

'I'll hold you to that,' he said, and watched her sashay away.

The Quinns were riding on their fine thoroughbreds up towards Lincoln when they ran into Sheriff Pat Garrett and Azariah Wilde coming fast their way.

'Just the man I wanted to see,' Quinn roared. 'We've had our house under attack by a gang of thugs led by John Dog Crandal. We need protection.'

'Anybody killed?'

'Not yet,' Kate screeched. 'But what do I have to do? Get raped and slaughtered before you act?'

'I'll call in on my way back. I'm looking into another matter. Top priority from Washington.'

'That's enough, Garrett. No need to tell the whole damned territory,' Wilde butted in. 'Come on. We haven't got time to hang around.'

When they reached White Oaks the Quinns booked into the Golden Garter. As they freshened up in the hotel's best room Quinn couldn't resist taunting his wife. 'So, you're still in love with your precious Logan, are ya?'

Kate ignored him but he could see her claws tense, her nails scratching the surface of the dressing-table. So he went on: 'It looks like we're gonna have to cut him in as a partner, then, don't it? You don't wanna lose him. And I ain't gonna find another feller who can run a stage line like him. Looks like we both need him. So, I'd better go sweeten him.'

'Where is he?' Kate asked sharply.

'I dunno. One of the saloons, I guess.'

First Quinn had to do business at the mine, then draw out $2,000 in gold from the bank. He deposited this for the night in the stage line office safe. He found Logan propping up the bar at the Four Aces, chatting to the croupier girl, Dawn Adamson.

'So this is how you waste your time,' Quinn chuckled, slapping him on the back. 'Tryin' to get in the pants of this dinky li'l darlin'?'

Logan groaned. 'What do you want, Quinn?'

'We've got an appointment at the lawyer's office. You and me. I'm making you a full partner in the stage company. You'll be in charge, run it the way you like. Come on, pal, let's go.'

'I ain't so sure I wanna be a partner,' Logan drawled, shaking Quinn's hand off his shoulder. 'You ain't even heard how we got attacked by that lousy gang of road agents.'

'Sure I have. Old Randy tol' me all about it. You'll both be gettin' a big bonus for getting the gold through. And you can name your own remuneration. Whatever the line will stand. Come on, Josh, no hard feelin's. Kate's told me all about your li'l, how shall I say, get-together, last summer. You played the white man and called a halt. Time to forgive an' forget. I'll see she don't bother you no more.'

'That's easier said than done.' Logan glanced uneasily at the girl. Then turned to Quinn. 'OK, from now on I'll play straight with you if you play straight with me. Kate and me... I'm sorry about it, Paco. It's a long time ago. It's over now.'

'Don't worry about it, Josh,' Quinn said.

'You can reorganize the line, buy another coach, hire relief drivers, whatever you like. Come on, I wanna head back tomorrow. I gotta meet Crandal.'

'You're gonna pay?'

'Yeah,' Quinn growled. 'But I'd like you along in case of trouble.'

'OK,' Logan sighed. 'It's a deal. Partners, it is.'

'Let's go over to the Golden Garter and celebrate,' Quinn suggested, when the contract was all signed and sealed.

Logan could hardly refuse to raise a glass to their success. 'You're not a saddle bum any more,' Kate said, in her husky tones. 'You'll be a man of standing in the community.'

'Listen to her,' Quinn roared, the whiskey already getting to him, not caring if everybody else in the bar heard. 'She married me for my money, because I provide her with everything she wants. And what gratitude do I get? She tells me she's in love with this other guy. Yeah, *him*. He looks like butter wouldn't melt in his mouth, don't he? So, I say, OK, go and live with him like some tramp.'

Quinn got to his feet and stumbled to the bar for a refill. He caught hold of a drinker's arm and laughed uproariously in his face. 'The big joke is he don't want her no more. He's fallen for some other gal. So Kate can't have him. She's stuck with me whether she likes it or not. She married me and I got her.'

'Is that right?' Kate hissed, staring at Josh. 'Who is she?'

'Ach, take no notice.' Logan got to his feet and shrugged. 'It's just Quinn. Drunk talk.'

'Where you goin', partner?' Quinn had returned to the table. 'I was gonna order supper.'

'I got someplace to go. Don't drink too much, Paco, we've all got an early start in the morning.' He stuck his Stetson on his head. 'Have a nice evening, folks.'

Kate watched him leave the hotel. Quinn

could see she was seething. 'Aw, gee, now look what I done,' he grinned. 'Frightened him off again.'

'Where's he gone?'

'Who cares?'

'I said where?'

'The casino. The Four Aces. He's got some young dame who runs the blackjack game. Strikes me he's crazy about her. Now, what are we gonna eat, darlin'?'

It was midnight. Kate, a hooded shawl around her, was in the shadows watching the casino. Eventually the tall figure of Josh Logan emerged. He strolled off back up the street to the livery where he was bunking. Kate Quinn watched him go. She opened her bag and checked the small Cloverleaf house pistol. It was an improvement on a derringer, lying snugly compact in her purse, its snubnose, two-inch barrel hardly discernible. And it packed a lot more power.

'Good evening, Mrs Quinn,' the bartender greeted her. 'Your husband's not here.'

'No. I'll have a glass of white wine.'

She examined the crowded gambling tables and spotted the girl croupier in a far corner. 'Good,' she whispered. She bought some chips and strolled over.

Dawn Adamson eyed her astutely. A bunch of gents around the table were just giving up the game, going to cash up. 'You lookin' to play, Mrs Quinn?'

Kate faced her and tossed down some chips. Dawn flipped cards, scooped the chips in. Kate tried again.

'I'm glad I've caught you alone,' she said, and took the Cloverleaf from her purse, concealing it in the wide sleeve of her coat. 'I need to ask you a question.'

Dawn looked into the deadly hole of the small gun that was pointed at her breast. Nobody else was aware of what was going on. She tried to catch the eye of the pit boss, but he had his back to her.

'Yes,' she said. 'What do you want to know?'

'Is Josh Logan in love with you?'

'I don't know.' Dawn hesitated, rattled. 'I don't mind admitting I'm in love with him.'

'You can forget him. Fast. I oughta kill you now, but I'm gonna give you a chance. I want you out of town, out of this territory. By tomorrow. If I ever see you again I'll kill you.'

'Why?' Dawn protested. 'What have I ever done to you?'

'He's not in love with you. He just imagines he is. How can he be in love with a cheap little saloon chiseller? That's all you are. What can he see in you?'

'Maybe I should ask him next time I see him?'

'Don't try to be funny. There won't be any next time,' Kate sneered. 'Remember there's four bullets in this. If I don't kill you with the first, I'll finish you with the next three. You better remember that the next time you walk along a darkened street.'

The two women eyed each other coldly for moments, then Kate tossed her chips down, stuffed the Cloverleaf away in her bag, turned and walked out.

TWELVE

Early the next morning Randy and Logan stocked up with shells for their rifles and revolvers, and made some purchases in the mining store, before driving the Concord coach along to meet Quinn. 'So, OK?' he called. 'Are we ready for a fight? Or are you going to pay the weasels?'

Quinn threw his hands into the air as he had them load a strongbox into the stage. 'Twenty *desperadoes?* We can't take them all on, Josh. There's only three of us.'

'Don't forget me,' Kate shrilled, joining them. 'I'm gonna be there to make sure they don't ride roughshod over you.'

'Ain't I told you it's too dangerous for you to be there?' Quinn growled. 'I said you're to stay here.'

'It's my house,' Kate insisted. 'And I'm

140

gonna be there come hell or high water.'

'Be it on your own head. I ain't arguin' with you. Come on, let's move. We gotta be there by tomorrow. *Domingo*, Crandal said. Sunday at noon.'

'Sorry, men, ain't taking no passengers today,' Logan told two miners who wanted to get on board. 'This is a private excursion. Just Mr and Mrs Quinn, the owners, riding inside.'

Logan climbed on to the box, cracked his whip to set the team moving, and gritted out to Randy, 'Whatever Quinn decides, I'm ready to play John Dog at his own game. Who knows, we might have a surprise for him.'

'Yeah,' Randy drawled. 'I cain't wait.'

When they got to Roswell they rose early and told the Mexicans to stay in their houses. Then they waited. That was what got to them, not knowing when Crandal would appear.

Kate had donned her split leather riding-skirt and hard-brimmed hat. She clomped about in high-button boots, a lightweight Pearson sporting rifle in her hands. 'What are you gonna do?' she asked her husband for the umpteenth time.

'Aw, I dunno. Leave me alone.' He had dragged his casket of gold pieces from the coach and dumped it on the parlour floor. 'What else can I do but pay 'em off?'

But Quinn was like a parrot with a sore head, talking constantly to himself, switching from one idea to the next, forever changing his mind.

'Why should I give them all my hard-earned cash?' he asked Logan. 'It ain't right. But I think I got to.'

Josh had checked his Colt Lightning revolver and was oiling his high-powered Thunderer rifle. He shrugged, peering out of the window. 'If it ain't right, why you got to?'

'Because he's a coward, that's why,' Kate sniped. 'He's terrified they'll blow us to kingdom come.'

'I ain't sceered. Tell her, Josh, it's the only sensible option.'

'Fear is a bad enemy. You gotta pull your-self together, Paco. Make your mind up. It's your cash. But you know my opinion.'

'Yes, Josh is a *man*,' Kate snapped. 'He's ready to fight.'

'I ain't no braver than the next man, I gave into 'em once,' Logan replied. 'Sometimes there ain't nuthin' else to do but stand up for your rights.'

'Good on you, Josh.' Randy was kneeling at the window, his Greener resting on the ledge. 'I smell gun-fightin' weather!'

They hung around glumly most of the day, trying to kill time. 'Maybe they won't turn up after all,' Kate remarked, as she made coffee.

Quinn tipped whiskey into his mug. He was already half-soused. He stood to go to peer from a window for the hundredth time. *'Christ!'* he growled. 'Here they come!'

They sprang to the windows. Logan knelt but did not show himself. 'Pull your rifle back, Randy,' he called. 'Let's surprise 'em.'

The line of bandits, all with rifles or carbines in their fists, came pounding towards them on their fiery mustangs, splashing across the streams, through the allotments, leaping over peasant carts, hauling in a snorting, stamping, menacing line before the house.

John Dog spurred Satan forward. 'We're here for what we're owed, Quinn. Bring it out an' there'll be no trouble.'

'He ain't havin' my money.' Quinn lurched to the door, his rifle in his hands. 'You lousy packrats can go play with yourselves. Get off my land.'

Quinn raised his rifle and snapped off a shot, grinning as John Dog's hat went spinning. He backed into the house. 'That showed him, eh, Josh? Who's yeller now?'

John Dog had swirled Satan around and scattered his men in all directions. At a safer distance he turned, his long black hair blowing across his face. 'That's the way you want it, Quinn?' He gave a shrill scream. 'Blast 'em outa there, boys.'

Suddenly they were all shooting at once,

Kate, Quinn, Randy and Logan, giving the *viciosos* a fusillade of rattling gunfire. One man was catapulted backwards off his bronco. Another caught a bullet in his back as he spurred to move away. 'Got him!' Logan cried, as his lead shattered a bandit's jaw in a spray of blood and bone.

The outlaws were galloping backwards and forwards, before and around the house. 'Cover the back, Randy,' Logan yelled. 'Don't let any of them jump on the roof.'

Everybody was yelling and blazing away, for he who hesitates is lost. Snap-shooting, ducking back, those inside had no time to think as bullets screamed and smashed into the walls, just to scramble up again, try to take aim as a rider thundered past, and shoot.

John Dog came pounding towards them on Satan, the lit fuse of a stick of dynamite fizzing in his fist. Josh, reluctant to bring down the fine beast, tried a split-second shot at his head. Crandal swerved away, hurling the stick. But Logan's reaction had made the throw go awry. A bedroom at the end of the house was blasted apart, instead.

'Two can play at that game,' Logan gritted out.

When he had visited the mining store in White Oaks he had bought a box of dynamite. While they waited he had rigged up booby traps at strategic points, running long fuses back to the house covered over by sand to disguise them. He leaned back and lit the first. He watched it go fizzing across to the foot of an old cart which several bandits were using as a vantage point from which To hammer bullets their way.

'Boom!' The cart went up and so did the bandits, limbs torn apart in a mess of rocks and splinters.

Others ran for cover as he set yet more fuses off, horses somersaulting as more explosions crashed out, men throwing up their hands and rolling away as the ground fountained beneath them.

Kate fired at one on the ground, making sure that he was dead. Logan glanced at her.

Like them all, she had the killer instinct in her eyes, the bloodlust that comes when the enemy comes in sight. She gritted her teeth and sent a Mexican *hombre* bowling over like a shot jackrabbit.

Logan grabbed for another dynamite stick, lit it, and when he saw John Dog galloping towards them again, hurled it towards him. But Crandal veered clear as it exploded in the air.

'Damn him,' Logan said. 'I'm going after him.'

Suddenly, he heard Randy, at the back window, cry out. He dashed in and saw him lying on the floor holding his abdomen. 'They got me,' he groaned.

'Hold on, old-timer,' Logan dragged him to one side. He whipped off his bandanna and tried plugging the wound. But it didn't look good.

The face of a moustachioed man, probably the one who had shot Randy, appeared at the window. He was trying to climb up, a pistol in his hand. Quinn blasted him on to his back and roared, *'Hijo de puta!* Try to kill me, would you? That's the only treatment you understand.'

'Cover me,' Logan said, and vaulted out of the window, his Lightning in his hand. He edged his way around the house and sprinted across the yard. A Mexican in a sombrero, carbine in hand, rose up from behind a pile of rubble caused by one of Logan's mines, and spat out a shot. Logan put a slug between his eyes. There was nothing to do but try to stay calm, ready to react. He took aim, fired at another who presented himself. There were bodies all over the place. But where was John Dog?

He prowled forward through the stream and trees, shooting twice more at adversaries, without success. Suddenly Satan was charging down upon him, John Dog swinging his machete. Logan rolled aside, got John Dog in his sights, but there was a dull click when he squeezed the trigger. He was out of lead.

It seemed Crandal was, too, for he had

stuffed his Remington in his belt. He had the razor-sharp machete in his hand and swung it viciously at Logan. It could have severed his head if it connected. But he dodged and dived as the blade swished back and forth. A chunk of his hair was trimmed as he was forced backwards into a deeper stream. Crandal spurred Satan at him. The stallion lost his footing on the muddy bank, slithering and kicking, and keeled over on to his side, pitching John Dog into the stream.

It gave Logan a chance to snatch up a discarded rifle to use it as a club as Satan floundered away and Crandal struggled to his feet, the machete still in his grip. Then they were locked in combat like two warriors of old, slashing and blocking and parrying, their weapons clanging against each other.

Quinn had lurched out in front of the building, firing wildly. 'We've won, Kate!' he shouted, elated by the heat of battle. 'We're gonna be OK.' He turned back to the house doorway where his wife stood. 'Just you and me, baby. We'll start anew.'

'You think so?' She was pointing the rifle at his chest. Snakily her eyes switched back and forth to make sure nobody was watching, but amid the drifting black powder fumes, the general mayhem, who would notice? 'Think again.'

A blank look came into Quinn's dark eyes, like a dog about to be whipped. He reached a hand out to her, pleading, 'Honey, don't do this. I'll make us rich.'

Kate squeezed the trigger, once, twice, three times and her husband stumbled from side to side, groaning, 'No!' He collapsed at her feet. She quickly retreated back into the house as the sulphurous gunsmoke billowed.

Down at the stream the two men were still locked in a struggle. Logan jumped back as the machete cut across his abdomen. He grimaced with the effort and caught the outlaw a mighty crack across his cranium with the rifle stock. 'Unh!' Crandal rolled his eyes and dropped the machete. Logan snatched it up and with all his strength sliced the blade into the outlaw's jugular. Blood fountained as John Dog screamed, and rolled back into the water.

Logan collapsed to one knee, gasping for breath, and watched his enemy's blood colour the sunlit whorls of the stream. John Dog was quite dead. 'Waal,' he drawled, as he got up, 'you can't say you didn't ask for it, pal.'

He waded across and tried to catch hold of Satan, but the stallion showed his teeth, whinnying and going up on his back legs, kicking out. 'Steady, boy,' Josh soothed, hanging on to him, seeing the deep spur scars in his sides. 'You remember me, doncha? Nobody ain't gonna hurt ya no more.'

Most of Crandal's mob lay in attitudes of death, others were moaning with their injuries, and yet others were climbing on to mustangs, making their escape, heading away across the prairie as though all the devils in hell were after them.

Logan led the stallion back and stopped,

surprised to find Quinn, too, laid out dead.

'He should never have showed himself outside,' Kate cried, pointing to the running men. 'One of those bastards pumped three bullets into him.'

She hugged the tall Texan to her. 'Oh, Josh, thank God you're safe.'

'Yeah, I'm safe enough,' he muttered, somewhat puzzled by Quinn's position, and easing himself from her. 'How's Randy?'

'You don't ask about *me*, if I'm all right. All you worry about is Randy. You and he are like an old married couple.'

'We been partners a long time, Kate.' He strode into the house but was glad to find Newbolt sitting up. 'How ya doin', fella?'

Randy forced a grin to his hard face. 'Guess I'll pull through.' He was still holding the blood-soaked bandanna to his belly. 'I been gut-shot afore.'

'Quinn ain't been so lucky. He's lying out there dead. So's John Dog. I'm gonna send a Mex'can fer the doc to attend to you. We need to get that bullet out. And, maybe, those outa Quinn, too.'

The villagers had crept from their adobes and were looting the bodies of boots, belts, whatever valuables they possessed. Crandal's gold teeth were prised out, an extra lucky find! The corpses would be hauled over to a communal grave and buried without ceremony.

Logan pulled Quinn into the shade so he didn't get ripe in the sun. He would, at least, get a headstone in the local cemetery. On an impulse he used his knife to dig out the slugs from him. Three smallish ones. Twenty-eights. The same calibre as Kate's lightweight lady's rifle.

She had brushed her hair and tidied up a bit, and was pouring them drinks when he went back inside. They had helped Randy into a bed in another room and were alone.

'Have some of Quinn's corn whiskey,' she said. 'He won't be needing it no more.'

'Nope, I guess not.' He took a swig from the tumbler and glanced her way. She looked so cool and confident. 'It was quite a fight. How did you say he got it?'

'Why worry about Quinn any more? He's gone. We're alive, Josh.' She raised her glass and gave him a dazzling smile. 'Now we're alone you know what I have to say.'

'Don't say it.'

'We have got everything, darling. Everything we ever wanted. We're rich.' Kate put the glass aside and stepped across the kitchen to hug herself into him. 'Oh, Josh. We can start to live again. Just like last summer.'

'What about Brad?'

'Brad?' The question flurried her. 'What do you mean?'

'Your winter driver. He's got a lot to say about you, Kate. It kinda surprised me.'

'Brad? You haven't been listening to him? He's jealous. It's all lies. Yes, he tried to come on to me. That's why we had to get rid of him. Who do you believe, him or me?'

'I'm inclined to say him.'

'Don't be like this, Josh.' She stared into his face as if in anguish. 'This is our chance.

Don't throw it away. I'm desperate, Josh. I need you. Help me.'

'This time I'm helping myself.'

'You mean that croupier girl?'

'Now I think about it, yes.'

'Don't be absurd. She's nobody. Just a cheap little saloon trollop. Have you gone out of your mind? What can she give you?'

'I dunno. But one thing I do know – I can trust her.'

'I can't let you go now. Not after what I've done for you.'

'What have you done, Kate?' He showed her the three bullets in his palm. 'Would these have anything to do with it?'

'Where did you find those?'

'Where do you think – in Quinn. You shot him, Kate.'

'Sure I killed him. I did it for us.'

'You're crazy, Kate. I never wanted you to do that. I told you a long time ago it was over 'tween us.'

'It ain't over,' she cried. 'I'll kill that bitch. She's not having you. I'll kill you, too, if you try to stop me.'

The lanky Pat Garrett stepped into the kitchen at that point, surprising them both. 'You won't be killing nobody, Kate. Not any more.'

Azariah Wilde joined him, officious-looking in his suit and derby. 'We heard everything. I am a lawman, too. Your words amount to a full confession. You will be charged with the premeditated murder of your husband.'

'Yeah, I'll gladly be a witness,' Randy called from the other room.

The law officers had heard the shooting as they rode towards the village. When they arrived, seeing all the carnage, they had proceeded on foot cautiously towards the house. When they heard voices coming from the open kitchen window Garrett had beckoned Wilde to pause and listen.

'I didn't say I murdered anybody,' Kate snarled, backing away, and pointing to Josh. 'It was him, Logan. He murdered him. He wanted our money. Don't you see? I'm the grieving widow here.'

'Save all that for the judge, Kate,' Garrett drawled. 'You'll git the chance to say a few more last words on the scaffold.'

'You lousy filth.' Kate pulled the Cloverleaf snubnose from a kitchen drawer and aimed it at Logan. 'You're the cause of this. You an' your *principles*. If I can't have you, that bitch you fancy certainly ain't going to.'

She squeezed the trigger and the .28 razored Logan's cheek as he turned his body instinctively away. She fired again, her face contorted with anger, but as she did so Garrett reached out a long arm of the law, grabbed her wrist and twisted her arm up. The slug splintered the ceiling. Garrett held her by her throat with his left hand, and disarmed her by superior strength.

'Hot damn, Kate,' he drawled. 'Take it easy. I'm gonna have to cuff ya.'

'Take your hands off me,' she screamed. 'I'll break you, Garrett. How dare you touch me?'

'Calm down, for God's sake.' Garrett snapped manacles on her wrists behind her.

'I reckon I'd better read you your rights to make this legal. Then I'm taking you up to Lincoln.'

Kate Quinn was snapping, snarling, spitting, luridly cursing and threatening them with hell. 'Let me go,' she screamed. 'You've no right to do this.'

'Sweetheart,' Garrett shouted. 'I got every right. You better get used to your new lodging. It's gonna be my jailhouse.'

THIRTEEN

When Josh Logan drove the stage into White Oaks, alone on the box and with no passengers, Dawn Adamson hurried over from the Four Aces, along with curious bystanders. Logan climbed wearily down and winced, holding his abdomen as a line of blood dampened his shirt.

'Josh,' she cried. 'What's happened?'

'A helluva lot,' he said. 'No need to worry. This is just a machete cut, courtesy of John Dog Crandal. It'll heal.'

'What's that burn on your cheek?'

'Aw, a present from Kate.'

He tried to push through the crowd but they demanded to know what was going on.

'John Dog's dead. Quinn's dead. Kate Quinn has been charged with her husband's murder,' he shouted. 'That's all I'm gonna

159

say 'til the trial.'

Of course, they were screaming and shouting, wanting to know more. He put an arm around Dawn's waist, more or less scooping her up, and pushed through to the Golden Garter. He clanged the bell for the manager. 'I wanna room,' he said, turning to her. 'Just want to git outa the way. You wanna come up with me?'

She hesitated, then nodded. 'OK.'

'What's your favourite tipple?'

'California white.'

'Right, that'll do. Make sure it's iced, mister.'

'You want a double room?'

His brow furrowed, questioning, as he met her warm brown eyes. 'I dunno.'

She shrugged and smiled. 'Why not?'

'Right,' he smiled. 'Make that tonight.'

When she slipped off the rustling silk dress and underwear she revealed a body that was neat-waisted and curvaceous, soft, warm and white as fresh milk. 'You're like an oasis in the desert to me,' Logan said, drawing her to him. She stood, naked but for her black stockings and gold crucifix on its necklace:

'You're not the first,' she murmured, as they kissed and caressed, 'but you're the first in a long, long time.'

And, as they rolled over on to the bed and made love, in spite of his wound, it struck him how easy and natural it was with her. They fitted together like two halves of a black-eye bean, as if they were made for each other...

'I was born into a world gone mad,' she told him over their candlelit dinner. 'The Siege of Corinth. My mother had brought me in when I was three years old from our place in the country for protection from the invading northern hordes. All I remember is the booming and whistling of cannon fire, collapsing walls, screams and shouts of terror. When the city finally surrendered we were starving and in rags and that's how it was for the rest of the war. Somehow my mother

161

kept us alive.'

Her daddy, too, had survived as the Rebs retreated, fighting desperately with the South Louisiana Cavalry to the inevitable end. He had returned, limbs and body intact, but somehow shattered in his soul. 'He had always been a gambling man, working the riverboats, from N'awleans up to Corinth, Memphis and St Louis and back again,' she said. 'When he had a big win we lived in clover. But when he lost we were back on the breadline.'

Dawn's mother died of a fever, and her father took her along with him on his trips after that. 'I was brought up in smoky, chandeliered salons, listening to the clicking of dice, sitting behind him, watching every card he played. It was a bit of a shock when I realized that the moves he made weren't exactly legal as he rooked the wealthy ladies and gents. Even more of a shock when they banned us from the paddle steamers along the whole of the Mississippi.'

'So, that's when you headed West?'

'He tried Dodge, Denver, Santa Fe. I was growing up by then, sixteen or seventeen, and an expert blackjack and poker player myself. Then there was some sort of trouble a month or so ago and we were moving south again. He had heard that White Oaks would be lucrative, but he made the mistake of stopping off at Fort Sumner.'

'Not a wise move,' Logan said. 'Those boys play rough.'

'Yes, and they sure don't like to lose. Two men, Charley Billings and Seth Smith, accused him of cheating and he was gunned down before my eyes. He's buried in the cemetery there.'

'Gambling ain't a healthy life style,' Josh mused. 'The dice are loaded against livin' long, 'specially in these parts.'

'He had that terrible addiction. He had to play on and on to the last throw. Me, I love to play the cards, but he certainly put me off cheatin' or losing my cash on 'em.'

'So,' Logan enquired, as he lit her cigarette and a cheroot for himself, 'who was the first one you mentioned? If it ain't ungentle-manly to enquire?'

'A mistake.' She smoothed back her thick black tresses and trickled smoke from her crimson lips. 'The spittin' image of my daddy, a handsome gambler man, but twenty years younger. I was head over heels with the two-timin' twister. But that was back on the boats.'

'I get the picture,' Logan smiled. 'So you ended up at Fort Sumner, down and out, with no place to go, and Peg Leg Fanny and her travellin' circus came along.'

'What was I to do? She said she was open-ing a casino at Stinking Springs and needed a croupier. Call me crazy, but I imagined that was all the job entailed. I soon found out it wasn't. Some casino!'

'Yeah, Peg Leg told me you lit out and why.'

'On the back of Clarence's mule. That black banjoist. He's with the orchestra at the Four Aces. A nice guy. For a former slave he don't have no chip on his shoulder, just lets the world roll along.'

They were interrupted by a reporter from the *White Oaks Advertiser* wanting to find out what he knew about the deaths of Quinn and Crandal. 'All I know is that Kate's been accused,' Logan drawled, getting to his feet. He glanced at Dawn and took her arm. 'C'm on, honey. Maybe we should have an early night.'

'That,' she smiled, 'sounds like a good idea.'

'We got a problem,' Pat Garrett told Logan when he rode in to White Oaks. 'Kate Quinn is looking for the sympathy vote.'

He handed Logan a copy of the *Las Vegas Gazette* with the banner headline: 'Quinn's Widow Hounded by Garrett.'

Mr Hieronymous Epstein, Kate's attorney, was reported to have stated at her preliminary appearance at Lincoln Court, 'This was a tragic accident, nothing more, nothing less.'

He described the incident when 'the

Quinns had been gallantly defending their home from attack by Crandal's merciless killers against overwhelming odds' and said, 'In the noise and confusion, amid the rolling clouds of gunsmoke, Mrs Quinn, not realizing that her husband had ventured outside, pointed her lady's rifle at a figure coming towards her. Before she could ascertain who it was the rifle accidentally discharged,' he said. 'She was appalled to see her beloved husband had been killed by her own hand.'

Mr Epstein proposed that the 'ridiculous and insulting' charge of first degree homicide be summarily dismissed. 'Surely this lady should be left in peace to mourn beside her husband's grave?'

Sheriff Garrett, who, it was said, had brought the charge against the widow of one of the territory's most prominent citizens, asked at this point, 'How does Mr Epstein account for the fact that I have three bullets taken from Quinn's body, fired by Kate Quinn's rifle?'

'We have only your word for that,' Epstein

replied. 'The word of a gunman notorious for ambushing his victims, like Charley Bowdre and William Bonney, who might well have been rehabilitated into the community, and killing them without warning, in Bonney's case in a darkened room, without giving him the chance to surrender. What kind of man is that?'

He added, 'In my opinion the sheriff is trying to cash in on his current, sensational publicity nationwide by bringing yet another attention-grabbing charge in his self-promoting bids for higher office.'

When Garrett objected to this, Epstein told the judge, 'This case has a very unsavoury smell about it. The sheriff's only other witness to back his claim that this poor woman – in a state of shock – admitted to the alleged crime is some ne'er-do-well drifter, a former employee, a stage-driver with a grudge against her.'

Making an application for bail, the attorney pleaded that the widow should be allowed to attend her husband's funeral and arrange his affairs, which she could not do in the confines of prison. 'This lady is of the highest moral character, has worked tirelessly beside her husband to build up this territory and to bring a civilizing influence to the rugged ways of southern New Mexico. There would not be the slightest risk that she would abscond.'

'District Judge George Beaney said that for the present, while investigations were concluded, the charge would stand, but granted Mrs Quinn bail until the trial in the sum of two thousand dollars,' the report concluded.

'I see what you mean,' Logan said, giving a scoffing grunt of dismay as he laid the *Gazette* aside. 'Kate's painting us two as the villains of the piece. The violins are certainly being played on her behalf.'

'You're not kidding.' They were in the bar of the Golden Garter and the tall lawman tipped them both a slug of whiskey from the bottle. 'In the past, judges and jurors round here have been frightened to bring in guilty verdicts due to threats of violence. Now they'll be sceered folk'll say they're hounding a poor innocent widder-lady. You can't win.'

'What about your pal in the derby? Ain't he giving evidence?'

'No, he's had to back out.' Garrett lowered his voice. 'Secret service. It would blow his cover. He's working around here on unearthing whoever it is has been forging them dollar bills.'

'Well,' Logan replied, savouring the liquor. 'Epstein's right in one thing. This whole case *has* an unsavoury ring to it. Maybe you should bury it?'

'What, and let that murdering bitch get away scot free? Don't you go backing out on me, Logan. You're my main witness.'

'Yeah? Well, Kate ain't gonna give up easy. She'll hit us with every underhand trick she can conjure.' Logan slammed down his glass and headed for the door. 'So long, sheriff. I got work to do.'

There was no way he could go on working

as stage driver for Kate Quinn, so he had tied up the loose ends, paid out the last of Quinn's expenses cash on hay at the livery for the horses, and suspended the service.

He had found himself a job attending to the broncos along at the Martinez corral. It didn't pay much but it would keep him alive.

Meantime, he had sent a letter with the fast rider, care of Ash Upson, postmaster at Roswell, for Randy, telling him to take it easy, and come on up to White Oaks when he had recovered from the gunshot wound.

Logan had had to move out of the hotel and lodge above the stables, which was where, later that night, Dawn Adamson found him.

'Looks like I'm down and out agin, don't it?' he muttered. 'I had hopes I might make somethang of myself with the stage line.'

'You're young. You've plenty of time. We both have.' As she lay in his arms on his blanket on the straw, and listened to horses shuffling below, she asked, 'What are you apologizing for? I don't mind.'

'What, the smell of a man who shovels horse shit?'

Dawn laughed and kissed him. 'I like you for who you are. Anyway, this is quite romantic.'

'Well,' he muttered, 'I had planned on asking you to marry me.'

'But'– she looked up at him, mischievously –'you don't need to now?'

'No, it ain't that. A man needs some sorta steady future, somethang to offer a gal if he's gonna git wed. I ain't got nuthin' to offer you right now.'

'If you're offerin' yourself that's all I need. So when's the happy day gonna be?'

Josh suddenly smiled, forgetting his troubles. 'Let's say a week. How's that suit you?'

'Suits me fine. And don't worry about cash problems. I got a good job and income. We can make do until you find your feet again, Josh.'

'I ain't got no intention of being a kept

man. I been thinking, when this business with Kate is over, of heading up to Colorado. They call it God's own country. We could homestead some land, build up our own ranch.'

'We could even,' she smiled, 'run our own hotel and casino, before the kids come along.'

'That's the last thing we need right now,' he muttered. 'Maybe one day.'

'In that case, if you're gonna make love to me, you better be careful,' she smiled, as he rolled her over into the hay.

But their troubles, for the moment, were not to be little ones. 'I've lost my job,' Dawn told him, a week later. 'The pit boss called me into his office, showed me two peculiar letters, one supposedly in the hand of Peg Leg Fanny, saying I worked as a croupier for her and absconded with a large sum of the takings.'

'And the other?'

'From somebody in Santa Fe I'd never heard of, claiming that I worked with my father as a gambling team, that we'd both been caught cheating and banned from the riverboats. And that more recently we'd been run out of Santa Fe.'

'It's Kate,' he said. 'She musta hired a private eye to dig up dirt. Those letters are obviously fakes. Whoever heard of Peg Leg Fanny puttin' pen to paper? She's trying to ruin us.'

'Unfortunately, the pit boss didn't think so. He said I was a security risk. He *did* offer me a job as a so-called waitress. Maybe I'll have to take him up on it.'

'No way,' Logan growled. 'You ain't doing that.'

'So, what shall we do, Josh?'

'I sure don't know. Guess what? Kate's accused me of stealing cash from Quinn and her. The two-hundred-dollar expenses cash. Garrett says she aims to haul *me* up in court.'

'She's crazy.'

'You're right. Mentally unhinged might be more accurate. But she's gunnin' for us in a very poisonous way, that's for sure. You got any savings?'

'Yes,' Dawn replied. 'Why?'

'I think you better take them out and go. We gotta split up for a while. Go someplace she won't find you. Back East. That's all she wants. To get rid of you.'

'But that would be giving in to her.'

'It ain't right you should suffer 'cause of me. I'll find you when this is all through.'

'No, I ain't going. There's only one way I'm leaving, that's as your wife.'

'It's you who's crazy.' He hugged her to him. 'But I love ya for it. I can't leave 'til I've faced down this charge of theft agin' me. I gotta clear my name. But you gotta git outa the firin' line, doncha see?'

'But how can I go? There's no stage out any more.'

'I'll hire a rig. We'll drive to Las Vegas. We'll git hitched there. Then you can catch the train someplace safe.'

'I *have* got an aunt in Kansas City. I *could* stay. But you make sure you write me.'

'It's a deal. It's you I'm worried about. But don't worry. Everythang'll be OK. I'll meet you in a month or so an' we'll be together again.'

'Good.' Dawn linked her arms around his neck, holding tight. 'I can't give you up, Josh. I love you too much.'

FOURTEEN

It would take them a good five days to drive the 250 miles to Las Vegas in the hired lightweight rig, even if they kept up a steady clip. It was wild, rough country and travellers were few and far between.

They reached Lincoln the first night and Logan called in the sheriffs office. Garrett told him Kate was pressing the charge of theft of expenses cash. 'I'm gonna grant you a bail bond in the sum of fifty dollars to appear at court here in ten days' time,' the lawman drawled. 'I'll trust you not to abscond. Kate's telling everybody who'll listen that it was you killed her husband, not her. There were no direct witnesses, of course, but when her trial comes up I'll stick by what I overheard. The trouble is the more she repeats them lies the more likely folks are to believe her.'

They had a few drinks in Rosie's saloon and bedded down overnight in Garrett's empty jail. When they trotted their pair of horses into Roswell the next afternoon Logan located Randy at the 'dobe of a Mexican family. He was sitting outside beneath a bamboo canopy, tugging thoughtfully at his moustache danglers.

'You're gittin' wed?' he beamed, when they told him the news. 'I'd sure like to be your best man, but I ain't sure I'm up to riding to Vegas just yet.' He had eased himself painfully out of his chair. 'This hole in my side's taking a while to heal.'

Logan slipped ten dollars into Randy's palm to cover his keep as they left. By then it was getting dark and he was keen to slip away without being seen by Kate, if she was home. 'Take it easy, old-timer,' he called out. 'See ya on my way back.'

They pressed on north along the Pecos as the moon showed. 'I feel like a fugitive,' Dawn said, as she slipped an arm through his. 'Like it's me who's to blame, not Kate.'

When he deemed the horses needed to rest they laid out on their blankets on the riverbank. Logan didn't light a fire for it was dangerous country. There were still plenty of ne'er-do-wells about who might not think twice about trying to rob them, or worse.

With the dawn they went clipping on, following the narrow trail across the prairie. He had planned to give Fort Sumner a wide berth, but when one of the horses lost a shoe Logan changed his mind. 'We'll have to call in at the blacksmith's there,' he said. 'We can't risk her going lame.'

He didn't like the idea, but what else could he do?

Paulita's pantalettes were dangling from one ankle as her bedsprings creaked and she hung on to Seth Smith. *'Mi amor,'* she groaned. 'That was beautiful.'

'Yeah?' Smith raised himself above her, sweat streaming from him, and grinned toothily in the half-darkness. 'I allus aim to please.'

'Don't worry,' the girl said, as they paused, listening intently for any sounds from her parents' room. 'Papa still snores.'

Seth extricated himself from her, dragging on his trousers and shirt. 'All that action's given me a thirst. I'm goin' over to Beaver's for a beer.'

'Darling, don't leave me,' Paulita pleaded.

'I'll be back.' Seth grinned. 'For seconds.'

'Please don't be long,' she moaned. 'Hurry back to me.'

The youth jammed his plug hat on his head at a jaunty angle and climbed out of the open window, not bothering to put on his boots, just picking up his Smith & Wesson, letting it hang from one finger as he strolled across the parade ground barefoot. He looked as if he didn't have a care in the world.

'Hi,' he called to Charley Billings as he sauntered into the saloon, bought a beer, and joined him. 'Wimmin'! Don't they cling?'

'Yeah.' Charley grinned. 'Funny how once ye've done it they don't seem so int'restin' no more. At least, 'til next time.'

'Ugly Dave' Richards had left Tom at the hideout and come into the fort to find out where they had got to. He glowered at them. 'No woman ever got me tied to her apron strings,' he muttered. 'You're crazy hanging round here. When we going to Mexico?'

'*Mañana, amigo.*' Seth gave him a reckless grin, raising his glass. 'Relax.'

'*Mañana!*' Ugly Dave spat the word with contempt. 'You're gittin' like the damn Mex'cuns, Smith. It's allus *mañana.*'

'What's the hurry?' Charley stretched out his long, leather-clad legs and eased the revolver stuck in his belt. He poured them whiskeys from the bottle. 'Nobody ain't gonna bother us. We left no witnesses.'

It was about midnight and the saloon was remarkably quiet, just a bunch of Mexicans swapping stories in one corner, another gently strumming a guitar, and three Anglos, harmless characters with whom they were familiar, sharing a bottle in another corner.

'True,' Seth said, placing his revolver on the table. 'Think I'll git me another beer.'

Logan drove the high-wheeled buggy through the gates of Fort Sumner in the moonlight, past the Maxwell house, and across the dusty parade ground to the smithy. The stable doors were closed so he roused the blacksmith from his living quarters. 'I'll pay double if you'll put a shoe on tonight,' he said. 'We're in a kinda hurry to get to Vegas.'

'It would mean rekindling my coals,' the blacksmith protested. 'It'll take an age. Aw, OK. You'll have to hang about.'

Maybe the sight of Dawn's proferred dollars made him agreeable. 'I'm starving,' she said. 'Is there anywhere we can eat?'

'Only Beaver's saloon this time of night.'

Logan frowned, pursing his lips. He didn't like it. Not the thought of going in there. Not with the girl in tow. But his stomach rumbled too, at the prospect of the sonuva-bitch stew – bits of all sorts of offal chucked in – that Beaver kept bubbling on his stove.

'Guess we can give it a try,' he drawled, sticking his thumbs in his trousers' pockets and setting off across the parade ground. Dawn swung along beside him, hooking her arm into his. 'But the sooner we git outa here the better it'll be.'

Moths fluttered around a hurricane lamp and the air inside Beaver's saloon was warm from the pot-belly stove and murky with tobacco smoke. 'What kinda vittles you got?' Logan asked at the bar.

The old saloon-keeper slid two bowls towards them and pointed to a cauldron on the stove. 'Help yourselves.'

'What have we got here?' Seth called mockingly from behind him. 'If it ain't the stage driver.'

Logan froze for moments. 'Shee-it,' he gritted out.

'Who's the purty gal?' Charley asked, his fingers playing over the butt of his revolver. 'Tasty, ain't she?'

Logan put his gun hand on her arm and

pressed Dawn aside. 'Keep well outa the way,' he muttered. 'This is 'tween me and them.'

He turned to face them, registering each one's position as the men in the room began to scrape their chairs back out of the shooting line. 'I understand you two killed this young lady's father,' he whispered. 'That weren't a nice thang to do.'

'What's he talking about?' Ugly Dave asked.

'The gambling man's daughter,' Seth recalled. 'Yeah, nice of her to come back. And you, too, mister. You got some grievance with us?'

'Walked right into a trap, ain't he? Knows it, too.' Charley Billings stood slowly and stalked away to one side, easing the fingers of his right hand, his eyes fixed on the Texan. 'Ever see a man look so sceered?'

Ugly Dave gave a caustic laugh, and got out of his chair, pulling his six-gun in its holster around from under his beer gut. He hitched up his gunbelt, moving away, preparing to strike. 'Say your prayers, pal. Don't worry, I'll personally attend to the li'l gal for ya. Hey, maybe we could sell her down in Mexico?'

'You cowards,' Dawn shrieked, from her position by the stove. 'Why don't you fight fair? Josh would willingly meet you one at a time.'

'Josh, is it?' Seth crowed. 'Ain't that sweet? Allus like to know who I'm killing.'

But he screamed as Dawn hurled the cauldron at him and the boiling contents hit him in the face. His Smith & Wesson was out as he staggered, but his shot went wild. And he hit the ground as Logan's Lightning thundered, the slug crashing into the youth's chest.

The distraction made Ugly Dave flinch, and blink stupidly, losing valuable moments before he squeezed a bullet from his six-gun. Logan ducked down on one knee and Dave's lead smashed into the woodwork of the bar. Logan made no mistake with his second shot, sending Ugly Dave backpedalling out of the open door.

But the Lightning was sent skittling from his grasp as Charley fired and his slug hit the steel cylinder of Logan's gun.

'You jest hold it there down on your knees, mister.' Charley grinned through the curling gunsmoke, his spurs jingling as he edged closer, and kicked the Lightning well out of range into a corner. 'And you, sweetheart, come over and jine him where I can keep an eye on you both.'

'You've won,' Dawn replied, her dress rustling as she stepped across. 'Leave us be. We'll go. You can't kill us both in cold blood.'

'Cain't I?' Charley's dark-hued face beneath his hat brim was set in a determined leer as he pointed his gun at Logan's head. 'Down on both knees, you bastard. You've asked for it. You've killed my buddies.'

'No!' Dawn screamed as a gunshot reverberated, jumping with shock, her eyes wide with fear. But it was Charley, the rugged frontiersman and killer, who suddenly twisted his body with a groan of pain, throwing up his hands and pitched to one side to lie prone on the dusty floor. Blood oozed through the back of his shirt.

Young Brad McNulty stepped forward from where he had been sitting with the other men, Logan's smoking Lightning in his hand. 'I wouldn't shoot a man in the back ... not normally,' he stuttered. 'But it weren't right. Three aginst one. Is he dead?'

'Better put another slug in him to make sure,' Beaver said, coming up from behind the bar. 'Charley was a tough old goat.'

As Brad did as he was bid Logan got to his feet and hugged Dawn to him. 'You'd better do the same to that ugly one outside,' he said. 'Me, I could do with a beer.'

Others of the men had made a dive for Seth, the lucky one brandishing his Smith & Wesson.

'Sling the stiffs outside,' Beaver roared, ''fore they stink up my establishment.'

He passed a tankard of beer to Logan. 'It's on the house, mister. That's a plucky gal you got there.'

Just then, however, there was the sound of a posse of horsemen drawing up outside. They were led into the saloon by a tall rancher, Old John Chisum. 'What's going on?' he demanded.

'Feller here,' Beaver said, indicating Logan, 'just cleaned out a nest of rats.'

'They're the ones we were looking for,' Chisum replied. 'They gunned down two of my boys, sold the stolen cattle to Murphy. We strung him up from his barn rafter after he told us who they were. Then we followed their trail.' He gripped Logan's hand. 'Much obliged to you, stranger.'

Logan winced, shaking his bleeding knuckles. 'I'd be a dead man,' he groaned, 'if young Brad hadn't intervened.'

The hunky Brad looked elated. 'He's the first man I ever killed.'

'Yeah? Well,' Logan drawled. 'I'll have my Lightning back now.'

'In that case you'd better share the reward,' Chisum announced, taking a wad of notes from his pocket and counting them out on to the bar. 'I put up a hundred dollars on each of those rats' heads.'

Without further ado he led his men back outside. They mounted their mustangs and rode off into the night.

'Waal, whadda ya know, things are looking up!' Logan split the cash, shoving one pile towards Brad, one wad into his pocket, and passing the third to Dawn, winking at her. 'That's yours, honey. You earned it.'

He finished his beer and settled down with Dawn. 'Looks like we've lost our bowls of stew. What's all that caterwaulin'?'

'Aw, it's that Paulita Jennings,' Beaver told them providing them with plates of ham, instead. 'She was crazy about that spineless snake, Seth Smith. She's out there tearing her hair out. Hey, maybe you should console her, Brad?'

'Not tonight.' The young man grinned, ruefully. 'She'd be likely to crack a branding iron over my head, the mood she's in.'

Logan finished his meal, pushed his plate away, stuck out his long legs, and studied his

Lightning. 'That advert of Colt's when I bought this gun said I'd have six trusty friends in times of trouble,' he mused. 'That's sure proved true these past weeks.'

'It all depends who's firing the gun,' Dawn said. 'That's what counts. And, although Paulita has yet to realize it, your gun has probably done her a good turn.'

FIFTEEN

In Las Vegas Logan smartened up, buying a dark-blue bandanna and light-blue shirt, polishing his boots and giving them a shine. Dawn was radiant in a dress of silver tulle and a mantilla as they stood before the justice of the peace in the city hall. Logan had tipped an old galoot a dollar to act as witness. They treated him to a few drinks in their hotel after the ceremony and he insisted on showering them with a packet of rice.

'It didn't seem much like a wedding,' Dawn said, as they climbed the stairs to their room for a late siesta. 'I always dreamed of a church one with lots of friends around.'

'Maybe we'll do it in style again some day,' Logan said. 'Soon as I've sorted myself out.'

'Still, at least I've got your ring,' she murmured, as she snuggled in the bed by his side and twisted it on her finger. 'It makes me feel good.'

'Are you happy now?' he asked, as he kissed her and held her naked body close.

'Of course, I always feel good with you.'

But, to tell the truth, both were saddened by the fact that too soon they would be torn apart.

'I guess it's time to get ready to go,' Dawn sighed, as it grew dark, hardly able to bear the thought of leaving him. But they were both agreed, and her train was due to pull out at 10 p.m.

Randy Newbolt had made a last-minute decision to try to get to Las Vegas for the wedding. But it was his first time back in the saddle, and, with the sun baking down as he rode north along the Pecos, sweat poured from him and he was forced to take several rests, feeling kinda whoozy. It was all over by the time he arrived. At the hotel they told him the newlyweds had left fifteen minutes before for the railroad depot. Well, maybe he could still wish them well.

It was a good walk from the hotel to the rail station and Logan strode along with Dawn in the moonlight as the big engine with its tall stack got up steam. There was a bustle of passengers climbing into the carriages for the journey back East.

Logan handed Dawn's valise to a porter, then they lingered for a final kiss on the track by the steps to her compartment. 'We'll be together soon, honey,' he whispered, huskily.

He still had her fingers in his as she turned away to board. There was the sound of drumming hoofs and at first he thought somebody had left it late to catch the train. A white mare was charging towards them along the side of the track. It was almost upon them before he saw a woman's grinning face beneath a black hat. She wore a billowing cape, and the gleam of a revolver could be seen in her hand. It was aimed point blank at the startled Dawn. Too late Logan tried to intervene. There was the crash and flash of the explosion as Kate Quinn squeezed the trigger, and rode on her way, screeching with witchlike laughter, to disappear into the darkness.

Dawn cried out with shock as she lay, collapsed, half on the train steps. She slowly slid down to the track, staring at him with horror. 'Why?' she pleaded. 'Why us?'

'Dawn, honey, you're going to be OK,' he soothed, as he held her cradled in his arms. 'Hold on.'

But he could see blood flowering on the breast of her tight-bodiced dress as she groaned, 'Josh, don't leave me.'

'I'll never leave you, sweetheart,' he whispered.

As he was riding towards the depot Randy suddenly heard a gunshot, screams, shouts of anger and dismay. Then, galloping towards him along the track away from the scene came a white horse ridden by what appeared to be a man astride, in a black hat and cape, a gun in hand.

'What's this jasper been up to?' Randy

muttered, raising his Greener. 'Halt!' he shouted.

But the rider charged straight at him, firing several shots that whistled past his ears. Randy could do nothing but reply. He levelled his piece with an iron grip and, from forty feet, his bullet blasted a hole through Kate Quinn's chest.

'*Hay-zoose!*' he hissed, as he knelt down and met her glittering eyes. 'Kate! I didn't know it was you.'

'You bastard!' She coughed out her blood. But the light in her eyes was fading and she was soon gone.

'Nobody wants to kill a woman,' Randy told the inquest two days later. 'But she looked like some desperado comin' at me in the dark.' He was relieved that the coroner absolved him of all blame.

Logan had sat for several days and nights beside Dawn's bed. It was touch and go. But gradually she pulled round and she could sit up and take some broth. He moved her to

194

the house of a widow lady who would be glad of a few dollars to nurse her back to health. She had lost a lot of blood but was out of danger.

In the meantime Logan had taken a job as a bartender just to make ends meet. It was a bit of a rough house so he had to quell any trouble, too. A right to the jaw generally sufficed. One day a boy gave him a note summoning him to the law office of Hieronymous Epstein. 'What the hell's he want?' he wondered.

'So, you're this character Logan I've been slandering in the courts?' The lawyer beamed at him from among his books and papers. 'No hard feelings. I was acting on Kate's instructions. Now, of course, all charges are dropped.'

Logan shrugged. 'So, what's this all about?'

'I've been sorting out the Quinns' affairs. Relatives popping outa the woodwork from all over the place. Their mining assets made them rich. However, that's nothing to do with you.'

'So, what is? I hope you ain't suggesting I owe 'em–?'

'No, not at all. It seems you were their legal partner in the stage company. It was never dissolved. So you now own the whole caboodle, offices, horses, and there's a new coach that had been ordered by Mr Quinn. You'll find it at your depot. It's been held in escrow. The corrals, the balance in the stage account, it's all yours.'

'Waal,' Josh drawled, 'you could knock me down with a feather.'

'I'd be happy to represent you, Mr Logan, take care of all the legal flapdoodle.'

'Sure, why not?' Logan tipped his hat over one eye and scratched the back of his head. 'It ain't the way I would have liked it to happen, but if Quinn's set me up in business I guess I ain't gonna look a gift horse in the mouth.'

Outside, he was still feeling pretty dazed, but he found Randy Newbolt and took him along to Quinn's yard. 'Ain't it a beauty,' he said. 'We're back in business, pal.'

The coach they were admiring was being given a finishing touch by a painter, so Logan gave him some instructions, then when he was done, a team in the traces, they drove the coach through the town.

'What's all the commotion?' Dawn smiled, as she rose from her garden chair.

'How you feelin' today, honey?'

'Fine. I guess I've been lucky. I feel really good.'

'You're gonna feel even better when you take a look outside.'

He blindfolded her and led her out to the garden gate, then whisked the bandanna away. 'Behold.'

'Oh, my golly!' Dawn stared at the spanking new Concord coach. Enscrolled on the door in gold paint was 'Logan Express Stage Lines.'

'I can't believe my eyes!' she cried. 'Does it mean it's yours?'

'Ours,' he said, opening and beckoning her inside. 'Fancy a ride?'

They descended at the town's best hotel,

the Golden Garter, and went inside to the bar. A bottle of sparkling wine was ordered and he filled their glasses, raising his in celebration. 'To us,' he said.

'We still got the deeds to the Leaning Ladder?' Randy asked, 'Ain't we?'

'Sure have. So ever we get tired of running a stage line we can go back to herding cows. Or do both.'

'Sounds fine,' Randy said.

Logan put an arm around Dawn's shoulders and gave her a squeeze. 'I got a postponed honeymoon to fulfill. How's that sound to you, sweetheart?'

Dawn hardly needed to reply. The warmth of her kiss said enough. 'I'm ready when you are,' she murmured. 'When's the next Pullman leave?'

'To us!' Dawn took a sip of the bubbly. 'Tell me I'm not dreaming, Josh. This has all happened so sudden-like.'

'You ain't dreaming, honey.' Josh encircled her waist with his free arm and kissed her lips. 'The wheel of fortune's spun lucky for us and that's the way it's gonna be from now on.'

Randy grabbed the bottle by the neck, took a swig, and gave a rip-roaring rebel yell. 'Yes, siree, that sure is the way it's gonna be.'

Just then the lanky Pat Garrett strode into the bar, looking even taller due to his high-heeled boots and Stetson, and called, 'Hi, glad to see you folks. I got some good news.'

He laid out a broadsheet copy of the *Las Vegas Gazette*, fresh from the press, with the front page banner headline, 'Sheriff Garrett vindicated', and the subhead, 'Kate Quinn's testimony proved to be a pack of lies.'

'Clap your peepers on this,' Pat said. 'We've made 'em all eat their words.'

'New Mexico rejoices today as the popular Sheriff of Lincoln County, Pat Garrett was proved to be the upright, truthful man-of-action we always believed him to be,' the report began. 'Kate Quinn's testimony against him has turned out to be a tissue of lies.'

Written by the editor of the newspaper himself, it stated, 'This loathesome creature, a harlot and liar of the deepest hue, not only murdered her own husband in cold blood, but gunned down Dawn Adamson, the young and pretty newly-wed wife of another hero New Mexico can be proud to have in its midst, stage driver, Josh Logan.

'It would appear that Mrs Quinn had the hots for Josh, but the handsome young Texan steadfastly refused her lascivious advances. So enraged was Kate that she went around spreading calumnies about the Logans, and even swore out false testimony that Josh had defrauded the stage company of 200 dollars. When such dastardly actions failed, Kate Quinn mounted her fine horse and made an unprovoked gun attack on the lovely and innocent young bride as she was about to board the train East. The evil attacker was shot dead from the saddle by stalwart frontiersman and stage guard, Randy Newbolt, as she tried to make her escape.

'The Governor of New Mexico has spoken

out not only in praise of Sheriff Garrett for sticking to his guns and arraigning Kate before the courts, but in praise, too, of Josh Logan and his friend, Randy, who risked their own lives to defend the Quinns' home at Roswell when it was attacked by John Dog Crandal and his gang of 20 murderous thugs.

'Not only did the brave Texan, Logan, kill Crandal in hand-to-hand combat, but he and Randy put paid to one of the worst bands of killers that have terrorized these parts since the demise of Billy the Kid.

'That, dear citizens, is not all. Josh Logan was himself responsible for killing the heinous Ephraim 'Scarface' Entwistle when that notorious ne'er-do-well Seth Smith and his boys tried to hold up his stage. He later faced-out this lowdown pack of rustlers and robbers in Beaver's saloon at Fort Sumner and shot dead Smith, and 'Ugly Dave' Richards, sending them to a richly deserved fate. The well-known young freight driver, Brad McNulty, came to his aid in the saloon, shooting down another notorious villain,

Charley Billings.

'New Mexicans can sleep more easily in their beds tonight knowing that they have such fine, upright citizens as Sheriff Garrett, Josh Logan, Randy Newbolt and Brad McNulty dedicated to finally cleaning up this territory.

'It is understood that Paco Quinn, although subject to bursts of boozism, as we all know, had done much to build up this country and provide his ungrateful, double-crossing wife, Kate, with all the luxuries a woman could expect, unaware that she was secretly a disgrace to the name of womanhood, and is believed to have lived a wanton lifestyle. It is further understood that he had made Mr Logan a partner in his company, and, on the death of the Quinns, Josh inherits it and will be operating the new stage line under his own name.

'Many will regret that this evil woman, Kate Quinn, could not have been hanged by the neck from a sour apple tree, burned at the stake, or, at least, imprisoned for life in a bastille on bread and water. Meanwhile, we wish the Logans good health and prosperity in running their new venture.'

'Whoo,' Josh yelled, after Garrett had read out the report word for word. 'That's some vindication. How did you get that editor to write such an abject apology after the lies he printed about us before?'

'Aw, them editors are all the same, hiding behind their desks and their highfalutin' words,' Garrett growled. 'I told the snivellin' li'l skunk that if he didn't I'd shoot him down like a dog. Publish or else!'

Garrett ordered another bottle as a photographer from the Gazette bustled in to take their pictures. 'This ain't gonna do me any harm at the polls for re-election,' he said, with his wide, gleaming grin, putting his arm around them to pose. 'What's more, I've heard from Texas that there's a thousand dollars reward due to you for killing Crandal, and five hundred each on the heads of Ugly Dave and Scarface.'

'Things are looking up,' Josh mused. 'You know, you're getting a tad old to be riding shotgun in all weathers, Randy. How about we put that cash to restocking the Leaning Ladder ranch and you run it as your own?'

'You mean it, Josh?' Randy beamed and blinked tears from his eyes. 'That's a dream. To have my own spread.'

'You deserve it and you can do it, pard,' Logan said, giving him a hug. 'Drink up now. It's time to celebrate. Here comes the whiskey.'

He had heard the thud of a barrel being rolled into the bar and it was none other than the strapping Brad McNulty. 'Waal, whadda ya know,' he yelled. 'If it ain't our other hero. Howja fancy driving the stage again, Brad?'

The young man grinned and asked, 'When do I start?'

'Tomorrow. I'm gonna trust you to take care of things while I'm away for a couple of weeks. Can you handle the new rig and take it up to White Oaks?'

'You bet I can, boss.'

'Be sure to tell Señor Martinez to hang on

to my hoss, Satan, and not to sell him. We'll be returning his buggy and pair in a coupla weeks time.'

'Why?' Garrett asked. 'Where are you off to?'

Josh pulled Dawn into him and kissed her lips again. 'We'll be kinda busy,' he said. 'We're catching the next Pullman to Kansas City. We've got a delayed honeymoon to catch up on.'

Dawn eyed him, astutely. 'Couldn't we have a proper church wedding first?'

'Sure. Go dig out the preacher, Randy. We ain't got no time to lose.'

By now, folks had read the news and word had got around. There was a big crowd for their wedding in the church and a bigger one when they rolled up in the stage with Brad and Randy on the box to board the express. Logan and Dawn stood on the rear platform as their Pullman pulled out. People called good luck and cheered as the smiling Dawn tossed her bouquet to the girls. Randy fired his Greener in the air and there was a general hullabaloo as Brad drove the new stage and six alongside the track for half-a-mile or so as the train rattled off.

'There goes a couple,' the sheriff said, as he stood among the waving crowds, 'who deserve to do well in this territory.'

Garrett, alas, didn't do so well himself. He lost his job in the ensuing election of sheriff for Lincoln County. He returned to Texas and joined the Rangers. Later in life, as he stepped down from his horse on a lonesome road, he was shot in the back by an un-identified assassin. Such was the Wild West!

This Large Print Book, for people
who cannot read normal print,
is published under the auspices of
THE ULVERSCROFT FOUNDATION